YOU Taught Me

DELANDA MCNAIR

You Taught Me:
Why You Should Want Welcome and Receive Your Second Chance.

Copyright © 2019 Delanda McNair

ISBN-13: 978-1-7329907-0-8 Print

Truly HIS Pen LLC

Published in the United States of America. 2019

Revised Publised in the United States Of America, 2021

Table of Contents

Father Then The Eyes Can See 5

It's Time 9

The Beginning 10

You Taught Me

Chapter One 11

Chapter: Two 34

Chapter Three 62

Chapter Four 85

Chapter Five 111

Chapter Six 131

Chapter Seven 142

About the Author 181

Acknowledgements

Again, to my family, thank you for being perfectly you and the role you each play in the making of, "the who," that I am and will unfold to be.

Mother, you truly are the example of the selfless, nurturing, giving woman that I strive to become.

Dad, so wish you were here, your voice and your presence are ever missed, thank you for giving me you!

You Taught Me

The follow up to *Father, Then The Eyes Can See*

Returning From: Father, Then The Eyes Can See

Guy and Samantha Shepherd, Daughter Grae

Mrs. Aria – Angie's Home Assistant

Kevin and Kathy Koole, Daughter Kaye

Stewart and Grace Adam, Introducing their twin Daughter and Son

Felicia, Janet, and Lynn – Office Assistants

George and Angie "Unjhoy" Patient

Trevor and Lydia "Peerless" Patient

Sarah Aakef

Mr. Sandosjuah

And

Introducing:

Kolin Koole, Kevin Koole's Twin Brother

———————— · ————————

It's Time

It took some time, and they experienced a few setbacks, but the Adam family found and made all of the necessary contacts and finally received all of the confirmations. All invited would be in attendance and it was an uneasy, thrilling yet exciting feeling.

The day had finally come, and of the six-invited guest, not counting the children, all were in place except Guy and Samantha. Stewart was becoming a little anxious that neither of the two main guests had yet to arrive. Just as that thought tried to set heavy on his mind there was a soft knock on the door. I will get it Steward advised as he headed for the door. Just as Stewart opened the door to see Guy standing there Grace called out for him. Hey Guy, come in and make yourself comfortable buddy, while I excuse myself. Duty calls he chuckles as he jogged off. Before Guy could clear the doorway, there was another knock on the door. "I guess I will get It", Guy offered as he stepped back toward the door. Guy opened the door to see Samantha standing on the other side. At that moment, it seemed that time had stood still just for him as he took in her astounding beauty; traveling back to the first time, he had ever laid eyes on her. Who is at the door Stewart asked now making his way back to the front of the house? Guys silence said it all and Stewart continued to the door to escort Samantha inside. "Okay, now that we are all here, let's eat!" Stewart advised as he softly tapped Guy on the shoulder heading toward the kitchen with Samantha in tow.

The Beginning

Now with everyone gathered and having had the meal blessed, the guest were all seated and enjoying their meal. Grace being "Gracely-Grace," had arranged name cards with each place setting on the table. The card had two questions listed for each guest to answer as an icebreaker to open up conversation. Though a little awkward at first, they were warmly and delightfully received. The answers refreshed some and enlightened others.

For the kids, the double feature was a success, such a brilliant idea to pick up those extra wireless headphones. This made it possible for the adults, and youngsters to both, spend the evening exactly as they wanted while sharing the same space. It was a perfect solution for both the parents, as well as the children.

Chapter One

You Taught Me

The Shepherd Family

Looming thoughts: "Right now, I feel so numb it is scary. I believe I could really hurt someone." Guy shared. Kevin sat listening in silence for a few reasons. One, he had never seen his friend this upset, two he knew that his friend just needed to say, what he needed to say, and three Kevin really wasn't sure of what he was suppose to say. This conversation was so not about him but it was a challenge to avoid the thought of what he would do if this were his current life story. As Guy's friend, a part of him was rising up too, but he worked hard and remained neutral, and managed to keep a lid on that, as well as his personal feelings. The person responsible for this had to be heartless and a complete monster, Kevin secretly thought. His heart ached for his friend, knowing what he had suffered, and endured over the past nearly, five years.

After hearing his friends' summary, it was still a lot to digest so Kevin asked if he could read the letter. Sure, Guy answer, it is over here on the table. Here, read it, Guy encouraged, as he handed Kevin the letter. In fact, you can actually go ahead and read it aloud. Because ain't no telling what I actually missed, when I first read it. Kevin reached for the letter and read aloud.

Now, having read the letter, Kevin felt worst then he felt in the beginning. He was on the verge of anger but was well aware that his anger had no place here. Okay, I am aware that this may be the last thing that you want to do, but I have to ask you to talk about this. Tell me your first thoughts, after you read this, and now, that you have heard it read, what are you thinking Guy? Kevin encouraged his friend.

Silence, flood the room as they sat there, and this would take some time, for up until this, point, Guy had spent his time reacting and focusing on what he was missing and had missed for all those year. He was focusing on what he did not have, and what he thought was gone. Until being asked this question, his vision was so obscured he felt justified to embrace anger, resentment and possibly revenge, there was indeed, a cost to pay for this, and it was going to be paid!"

Once again, Guy found himself straddling thoughts of a past offense. "Ugh! I really need to be over Angie's decision, and actions, as well as that letter she sent me. Melt, remove and erase these thoughts God, I want it in the past and behind me so help me let it be."

Determined, to not be stuck in that heavy dark day from his past was a daily battle. Although Guy had made the decision, to stand firm upon his decision, to log this offense in the past and leave it there, the letter seemed to, hauntingly, attack his mind. Often he went back to that day, the day he read the letter, and shared the contents of the letter with Kevin. Now today, as if it had just happened, fresh in his mind, everything about that letter, and their prior discussion totally played out in his mind, yet again.

"Okay Guy, you cannot keep reopening, and revisiting, those raw feelings and emotions. It is the setup for a trap, and a distraction from your true goal. It is a new day, and you have new opportunities before you. HE has given you a second chance, a second chance at life, and a second chance with your family so use it wisely. Be wise, smart, alert, aware and in tune, as well as in touch. Okay, focus on your second chance Guy." He encouraged himself. This time around, he would learn what it takes to make it happen and openly and willing, be bold and intentional about family and love, as well as matters of "her heart." Your heart," he continued with his self-check and reminder.

"Um, matters of her heart. Her heart is my heart, but maybe that was not so obvious before all of this happened," he spoke through still tears.

Guy silently thought over his short-lived married life before that unforeseen evening at the hospital. With this seized opportunity, no matter how challenging, he made a self-declaration to do all that he could, which was necessary, differently than before.

Now trying to get his mind out of this dark memory Guy decided to say a quick prayer, "GOD, please equip and prepare me as you shape and mold me for this season. Help me to be the husband, the father the friend, my family and love ones need for me to be. You and I both know my track record is not that great so I am going to need a lot of patience and assistance here." "Oh, and PS: "GOD, will you tell her to call me, or should I ask that, you please have her call me? Psalm 84.11 reminds me that no good thing will You withhold from me, I know I did not walk right before you the first time around, but I am learning a different walk now God, and you already know that she is my good thing, so will You, "help a brotha out?" Oh, and remember that I am still learning how this, "God-talk, and prayer thing" works, so thank you in advance for your patience during this learning curve. Wait a minute. God you do know who "her" is right?"

"Relax Guy, just keep it simple he softly voiced and reminded himself, let's not get tripped up here." Okay, God, I need a do over, I want Samantha to call me. I want us to talk, please have Samantha call me, and please grant us some much needed, seized talk time, with effective, open and honest communication. Yeah that's better, okay cool. I mean, Amen.

Samantha's Thoughts

Thinking back over prior months, and with so much going on, and so much to face, Samantha felt like she was, caught in the middle of the unfolding, of four different life chapters, with all four chapters, playing out, in the same exact space and time. This was her life, but she felt like she knew little to nothing about the lead character or co-star.

"How could one have so many "life" question marks, and how could one live a balanced life from such a place of imbalance? What would allow one to be, or to feel justified to script out someone's life like this? If she was in a different state of being, and minus the recent near death scare, it would be so very easy to be angry with her right now, she thought. "I am almost angry with myself for not being at ease about, simply being completely angry with her," some of her thoughts continued. Ugh! This is not right, and how am I supposed to figure this out? How am I supposed to navigate this one? It has been close to five years now, and that is a long time and a lot of life's unfolding, for it not to have been truly lived." I have been living in a lie; huh, I have been living in a lie. What is truth for my life and how am I supposed to recognize it from this point on? Thanks to someone else's choices, I am now left in the middle of a life puzzle that someone else began, and have since discarded the box, leaving me to guess and figure it out. "Just figure out the completed picture why don't you, never mind the fact that you never saw the box cover, and have no clue as to what to expect, the finished product to be or look like."

"Great!" Just great, Samantha continued with her verbal thoughts. Okay, this is entirely too much, and right now I do not even want to think. I am going to bed, "and will you pllleeeaasssee settle my mind enough that I can go to sleep; I mean come on God, I didn't do this?" She asked and spoke, looking upward as she headed off to bed.

The day of the gathering, at Stewart and Graces, Samantha accepted Guy's contact information, but what was she gonna do with it? Would she use it, was she gonna call him? Wait a minute why should she call him, and was that even proper? Nah, he need to be the one calling me, she spoke a loud as she discardingly, tossed his written contact information to the side. However, before she could completely embrace that thought and move on, it dawned on her that she never offered or shared her contact information. "Great, now I have to be the one to call, she spoke. Who told him to place the ball in my court?" I do not know if I want possession of the ball. Wait a minute, what is up with the "sport" talk; I cannot remember the last time I even saw a game she spoke as a smirk peeked through, finding its place on her face.

By now, all of this eternal back and forth conversation brought a full smile to her face. "Got to admit, this is a little exciting", and with that thought still fresh and hot on her mind, Samantha took a deep breath squared her shoulders and dialed Guy's number. When she got his voicemail, she left a short, direct yet polite message and hung up. Why was I nervous about calling she thought? "Well someone blow the whistle because the ball is in play. Nervous or not, game on," she spoke aloud with a playful chuckle.

At The Office ~ And Reconnecting The Dots

Outside of Guy's mind adjustment, "surrounding most things, Samantha and Grae," things at the office were moving forward at full steam. Guy, Stewart and Kevin formed small groups for different tasks and targeted goals as they moved forward on current and new projects. The entire staff worked together as a unified body and life at the office was positively productive, and good.

Now I Get It. In the beginning, Samantha and Guy talked a lot more on the telephone then face to face. Being fearful this was all he could get her to agree to Guy made himself content with it, but these telephone conversations only enhanced his appetite, his longing and desire to see her. To converse with his wife, to be in her presence having the conversation take on a life of its own, and freely going wherever it chose to go. Now that, would be priceless right about now, he thought to himself. To be able to engage in, "face to face, give and take", communication with Samantha was both, greatly missed and needed.

If it were possible, Guy would have pressed the life "pause button," that day, when he opened Stewarts' front door, to see that there she stood. But he realized, it wasn't that simple, and he still didn't quite understand why in passing, she simply spoke to him like a comfortable acquaintance, instead of a wife to her long awaited, returning husband.

Therefore, though it was not what he wanted, the telephone calls were probably the best thing for right now, because whenever he sat across from her, he couldn't stop himself from staring, and because his expectancy was so thick in the air, each time they shared the same room, it of course, made Samantha very uncomfortable. God help me to respect her space and to grant her the room and time that she needs. Guy quietly prayed, and thank you in advance for future face to face conversations. He sighed as he set back in the chair wondering if and hoping, that Samantha would soon call.

On Her Way Back To Grace

Thoughts of the last gathering they hosted warmed Grace's heart. Since giving birth, Grace noticed that, although she was not exactly the same; that she had been smiling a lot more since that gathering. Maybe now she was open to actually talking to someone about the way she initially felt, after childbirth. When her husband originally offered this suggestion, Grace was instantly offended, almost to the point of rage, which confirmed to her husband that something deeper then exhaustion was going on. Thank God it was a different day, and though she was not completely back to being herself, Grace was more aware of how easy it was to disconnect, shutting everyone and everything out in the process. Recognizing this, Grace chose to do what she needed to do to beat this. She was not going to park in that dark place. Maybe it actually was something to Stewart's concern. After all, as always, he did have her best interest at heart. Where had she gone in the passing months? How did she get there, and how did she not see or sense herself heading there?

"What happened to me God?" Grace sadly and softly voiced. Lord, bible writings remind me that You will never put more on me than I can bare, and since I know you can do anything but fail, I am asking and praying for you to fix this, fix me and anything else in need of repair thanks to, or should I say "no thanks to," me. When You do this thing for us, I promise to give you; and you alone, all of the glory, honor, and praise. Right now, at the end of this journey, and all along the way, I am going to need You. We need you now Lord, we need you now!

Stewart Can No Longer Ignore The Weights Of Life

Stewart had returned to work but it was only for half days. Even when he left the house on workdays Stewart had been packing up the twins and taking them to a makeshift nursery he had constructed in his office, daily the nanny would meet him there to care for the twins, either Stewart or one of the partners volunteered to step in when the nanny needed to step away. Since the day the twins came home, Grace had never been alone with them because Stewart had always been present. Having it be this way for some time now, Stewart was not sure he would ever leave her alone with them.

It was not obvious to most, but Stewart was growing mentally, emotionally and physically exhausted. However in his mind, the way he felt had no place and it did not matter, for life would carry on this way until he had spent every part of him, if it had to. Sometimes he would smile within, as he imagined God gathering in all of the heavenly clouds, using them as stuffing for His ears, to keep from having to hear Stewart's earthly voice, and sometimes his cry. Though he was mostly a positive person, at this particular moment life was extremely weighty. It was long past time, for him to simply release, let go, and let God. He at least, needed to, allow his shoulders to drop long enough for all of the pain and heaviness, to roll off. Stewart needed to let go of the idea that he had to be strong, because though it was not an often occurrence, right now he just wasn't!

These had become the topics of focus during his still and quiet moments, those moments for he and God, "Lord when?" he softly spoke. "I know we spoke about this, but when?" he continued. He had been going strong, not missing a beat for what seemed to be a long time. After dropping his shoulders, he was unsure as to if he could un-pause this moment and square them back again, to continue on with the responsibilities of life, as needed and in the way that he had become so accustomed to, as of late. "Man, family takes two and then some," he thought. Stewart was supposed to be getting some work done but realizing, right now, that was not happening, he decided to release himself from the guilt of unproductiveness, to take a walk and stretch his legs a little. It was time for a little change of scenery, so he decided to go interact with others for a bit.

He was able to reflect upon a few verses that he had become familiar with some time ago, long before meeting Grace. "God has not given us the spirit of fear, but of power, and of love, and of a sound mind" 2 Timothy 1:7… "Except the Lord build the house they labor in vain that build it…" Psalm 127:1. "Ask, and it shall be given you; seek, and ye shall find; knock and it shall be opened unto you. For every one that asketh, receiveth…" Matt 7:7-8. In his mind, he was bible hoping all over the place, from the old to the new, testament. Lastly, his mind landed on, 2 Timothy chapter 2:7 "…and the Lord give thee understand in all things." Ump, **understanding**, and right now I need every ounce that you can spare God. I need it God, and I need it now.

Okay God, I am gonna go ahead and be honest, because you already know anyway, but sometimes I really do, not like her. Now that I am here, I do not know if I can, or even how, to turn off, this "I do not need Grace", survival mode attitude, but I know I need to. Better yet, I want to, but is that safe to do right now? When will it be safe to do this, how will I know when she is back? Will the Grace that I stood before you, family, and friends, saying "I Do" to, will she return, or will she surface as someone else? God I need you to shift my attitude and mindset back to a place, point and time when we truly were, "We!" Withholding nothing, choosing to be, spent upon "God; the marriage relationship and family." God, I want togetherness, I, we need that. We all need that type of atmosphere here in our home. Please hear me Lord, and move on us, Father we need it now.

Giving To Get Back To Grace

Though she was not completely comfortable with the thought of it, having acknowledged that something was not right, Grace took the second step and called in an appointment. Though awkward, and even though it was a rather small step she felt a little lighter.

Grace went to her babies' room to check on them, only to find the room was vacant. Wait a minute, she spoke wondering for a brief moment the whereabouts of her precious little ones, "um, that's right they are with Stewart." Grace recalled. Feeling a little lonely and unneeded, Grace headed for the kitchen. One of her most treasured rooms in their home. For Grace, it was a place of creation, a place of peace, laughter and fun. Though she sat silently in the kitchen, mostly everything else about her was full volume. She had been there the entire time, but not. Again the same question seem to plague her mind, "what has been going on with me, how can I feel so cold and distant?" Well, thanks to her patient and loving GOD, as well as her faithful husband, she now willingly, embraced and welcomed the chance to get the answer to this question, along with a few others. It was time for answers, and Grace was now ready to receive them.

The longer Grace set their alone in the kitchen, with their being no need to attend to, and no specific thing for her to do or focus upon; the more detailed and clear were her thoughts.

"Wait a minute. Why are my babies leaving with Stewart every morning like they are reporting for work?" "Whose idea was this?" "Hold on, who is taking care of my babies?" Grace spoke firmly as she reached for the telephone.

The day had come and off to the first session Grace went. Now with session one behind her, Grace was in route to meet her dear friend Kathy. Outside of the dinner party, this was the first, "one on one" time spent since Grace gave birth, and right now, she was experiencing mixed emotions.

They were emotions of excitement, embarrassment, disappointment and joy.

Real Talk With Kathy

With a table conveniently positioned near the window, Kathy headed for the door when she spotted Grace, now parking in the lot. Though a little concerned at first, Grace was very excited now, being able to see and reach out and touch Kathy, it was true medicine for her spirit.

"Grace Adam, I am so excited to see you girl, and look at you, as lovely as ever! How are you and how are the little ones? Wow Grace I have lots to share and lots to ask. So much so, that I do not know where I want to begin. Wait, what about you, where do you want to start" Okay wait again, I am so rambling right about now. I tell you what, I am gonna take a moment to breathe, and you just pick a starting point. Wow, I am sitting here with "my Grace!"

"Okay, let's see. Well you know I had mixed emotions on my way here right?" Grace offered. "What?" puzzled "why is that Kathy asked?" Kicking off with Grace sharing her thoughts and explaining her why, there much needed time together began. Kathy and Grace had a lot to talk about, and they did a great job of catching each other up on current life positions and status.

So wait a minute tell me Grace, what are your thoughts on Stewart hauling your babies off each morning? Kathy asked, now silently waiting for Grace to respond.

"Having come more to myself, and feeling more in tuned to my children and their need, I do not like it. It seems that if; they are alone in my care, that he is concern for their well-being. I feel questioned as a parent and mother. I love him, but I do not like him that much these days." Grace answered.

Wait a minute. May I ask why you do not like him right now? Kathy asked trying not to chuckle. "He goes behind me whenever I do things with or for the children. He reminds me, more like instruct me, of the "do's and don'ts, "whenever I leave the room in response to an, out-cry. He even offers, the same line of helpful advice, when I simply check in on them. It feels like, I am being watched. He acts like the only wise and capable parent in the house. The way he acts encourages me to simply be silent around him in fear of what may actually come out of my mouth if I am not silent." Grace continued. "I know that I am preaching to the choir so-to-speak, with what I am about to say, but you know you got to tell Stewart this stuff right? Why haven't you told him this stuff, why don't you just invite him to one of your appointments, include him in on one of your sessions." Kathy asked suggestively. "You know that I so do not like you right about now right?" Straight faced and emotionless, the once carefree and full of laughter and fun, Grace responded with a sharp side-eye look. Um, well only because you just informed me, Kathy responded softly yet directly as she allowed a little silence to fill the atmosphere. Grace you may not like me to much right now, but you will love me forever because you know I will never withhold the truth from you, as your true friend I have to tell you what needs to be said and we have to address the easy as well as the uneasy. "Grace Adam, I love you still, even though you just told me that you so do not like me."

Come on now Grace, I love and respect you, not only do I want you and your family to live out a blessed life full of Gods best, I expect it to be so. I am aware that it could unfold differently from what I think or expect, based on HIS way, thoughts and views for you and your family but it will not stop me from, at least putting my prayer and request in. Even if it works out a little differently, certain life chapters may be a little more challenging to live out than others are, but this holds true for any of us. Just always, know that I and the rest of the Koole family are here for you. We are here for all of you. We will listen, encourage, pray, cheer, labor; whatever you see fit for us to do to best assist you in moving along and truly living out this unexpected life chapter. I can almost see how a few of my suggestions wouldn't be immediately embraced but as your friend, someone that care about you, and love you, that fact means, that when necessary, that I get to say the thing and or things that are sometimes not the easiest to say. Please consider it, and try to be open to that which may be a help or beneficial for you, your husband as well as your children.

Sweetie, during this visit you mentioned the need of your children a lot. I just want you to embrace the idea that your husband "likewise," need that same kind of drive, focus and commitment. I am not even sure that he truly gets the dynamic of the changes, or of the effect, and of his feelings for having to wear both the hat of dad and mom these passing months. Again, I share this in love and I realize there are many details that only you and Stewart know, mainly you for right now, but I know that you are working on you and I am proud of you for choosing to do so. I cannot began to imagine the possible challenge of the work you have ahead of you right now, but in doing so, please do not allow that to be a conscious or unconscious, justified excuse to leave your husband out. Keep him in the loop; keep him abreast and up to date with your progress and any future unfolding surrounding you. During this time, it is so important to you, to him, and your family, and that includes us too.

I cannot say it enough Grace, we love you, and need you whether you want us to or not. No matter how unlovable you may think you are, or actually may be at times, Kathy finished in a softer tone and voice with a playful nudge and chuckle.

Grace caught it all, down to the smart ending, but since she was in "listen mode," a quick shift of her eyes said it all and they both smiled once their eyes met. The rest of the afternoon Kathy and Grace, both took turns, talking and listening, and at times even crying, they remained honest yet respectful and compassionate and everything shared was both needed and well received.

Driving off, to their different destinations, once their gathering ended, they both were refreshed, encouraged, empowered and for Grace, more open and in tune to the possible difficulties or struggles for Stewart during this time and the abruptly shifting of roles. During her drive, it was a time of self-checking and reflecting, and Grace had to be honest with herself. Though she was still feeling, "some kind of way" about her husband, and regardless of whether she loved him or not, just how open would she be to allowing him to take part in one of her sessions. This one was raising a question mark.

"Um, I am going to need a little more time on this one, Lord you are really gonna have to continue to help me along with this because honestly, no matter how right I know it is, I am not as open and receiving as I want to be. Oh, and if I should, or rather, if I need to include him on one of my session, You know that You are gonna have to do it right? I'm just saying, Grace spoke softly with a sigh. Because I honestly do not know if that is something I can do, and sadly, that is probably because I know, that is exactly what I should do. "Whew!" She released in a breathy sigh.

Grace Gets Real With Grace

"Okay God, I want my babies' home. Tell me what I need to say to Stewart because I think, that he thinks, the children are safer with him. Could he be right about this, are my children not safe with me God? Will you show me, allow me to see what he see, "or don't see" that makes it so easy for him to pack up the children every morning and cart them off to work with him? God, I am changing and I know for a fact that I am getting better, I want to be a parent, and I want to be a mother to my beautiful little blessings."

Grace set a little longer in quiet silence. In that very moment, her heart, mind and spirit was at peace, and her world was calm and still. She was ready to seize, "the now," and starting that afternoon, upon Stewart's home arrival, he would see and feel, firsthand, the home atmosphere he was accustomed to, one that he use to look forward to coming home to. The home life he and Grace had cultivated long ago.

Stewart Chooses Compassion Over Hostility

In the passing months, Stewart had been praying and talking to God a whole lot more. Even with already being one of prayer, he was aware of his almost desperate state of being, and his knees surely felt the difference.

He was glad Grace had found someone she was comfortable enough with, to actually committee to the initial three month, observation session. He was proud of her for being open to the session, and she appeared to be adjusting, and actually looking forward to her projected three-month review. Her actions showed and proved that she was serious about not parking in this dark place. It proved, that she was open to carry out the necessary visits to help usher her to a place of release, back to a nurturing place of, healing, as well as a place of mental and emotional health. For the most part Stewart was encouraged to continue to hope and believe in and upon God to restore that which was in need of repair and restoration, but it was still a lot that he did not know. Grace was talking these days yet silent still, and sometimes more formal than personable, even when she was at home with the family.

Stewart tried to get her to talk about where she was, how she was feeling, what she was thinking and how her sessions were going, but Grace never encouraged the conversations, and when she would answer, they were mostly short or very closed ended responses. Often Stewart fought off buying in to the thought, "if it isn't one thing it's another," though it would attempt to invade his positive outlook and way of thinking he refused, to let that thought come in and park. So once again, he had yet another thing to pray about.

The Patient Family

It had been more than 12 months, and in a few short days, her office mate would be returning to work. The doctor only signed off on light-duty for now, but even still Sarah. Aakef was looking forward to her office-mates return. She gave thought to a sweet way she could actually say it with an office gift but had made no decision as of yet. The more she thought on it, the more excitement she felt.

As always, throughout the unfolding of each stage of life with his wife, George had been, and remained, an honorable man. Both before, and after the "I Do's", however today, he truly felt tested. He and his, best friend, fiancé, and now wife never discussed her returning to the workforce. In his mind it was a given that she would be in the home, that she simply would not want to return to work. Family would become her new career focus. Moreover, having a little one so early on in their marriage, made it even the more so, a given to George, that is. As he pictured it, his wife would be home with their little one, and together, the two of them would love, care for and nurture their new family unit and relationship. Though he knew it was necessary, he was not looking forward to having this conversation with her. And if he would stop long enough to think about it and be honest with himself, it would be hard to decide which he was more bothered by; the fact that it was a topic that had to be discussed, or the fact that he only knew about her intentions by way of a few, overheard, passing conversations?

With she and the baby now both safe at home, Angie's, was not, the only work schedule that needed to be discussed, what about George? Was he going to return to his normal work schedule, if so, why? Even before becoming a husband and a father, why was he working anyway? Ump, that is a good question, he thought aloud. So what am I going to do? He continued on, in his verbal thought. Guess this is something I need to pray about, he spoke softly.

George and Angie had not spent much time discussing daily care for their little one, because once again in George's mind Angie would be a homemaker. With her recent medical scare and now being, "an unexpected" parent, why would she go back to the workforce now? Besides be it now or later, she had to know and understand that she did not have to return to the workforce, or was that too, something else George needed no help in assuming. Ump, they really needed to talk!

Today, George, Dad and the little one had breakfast plans and who knew what other unfolding would take place.

The Patient men had a wonderful day. Dad felt extremely blessed to see and hold a third generation Patient child, one to carry on the family name. His Georgie had changed and grown so much over the passing months. From him getting married, then standing with his Dad as he too got married, becoming a stepson, being able to live through a serious family health scare, and surprisingly becoming a father, required a lot of adjusting. It would change anybody, either for the better, or in some cases, for worst. Dad had always been proud of his son, but being able to see George be a father to his first grandchild was priceless.

Dad, where did you go just now, you became extremely quiet, all of a sudden. You know what Georgie; life is about service son. That is right service; service to others, and service to God, of course not necessarily, in that order but you get what I am saying. It is a sad shame to think that somewhere out there someone will go to their grave having missed that understanding, that reality and all of its opportunities.

Even with the early and unexpected death of your mother, we truly are a blessed family. I know assuredly that, she would be greatly pleased with you right now. With your choices and accomplishments, you make us pleased son, we are proud of you. No role or responsibility in this world could truly come close in comparison to parenthood. I thank God that you will now know and experience this first hand, yourself.

So how are you kids adjusting now that everyone's home and things are somewhat beginning to have some sense of normality? You know Dad, what a timely question. I was just quietly reviewing a few things a few days ago, and to be honest I think Angie should be a homemaker but I do not want to, just tell her that. I also thought about my career, and to be honest I could not think of a justified reason as to why I still report to someone's job every day.

Thanks to mom and auntie, and of course you, and your wisdom, right now the next three or four generations of Patients, never has to work a day in their life if that is what they so choose. Nevertheless, even with that being a fact, it is somewhat hard to say that I am ready to resign. You mean, *"retire* from the tradition nal workforce", Dad corrected. Yeah, that George replied with a chuckle.

Well, let us just say that if Angie decides to leave the traditional workforce; do you have any alternatives or suggestions to offer her? Son, I could be wrong, but having worked most of her life, Angie does not come across as the kind of woman, looking to quit work, come home, raise a child, and just live off hubby's stash. She is a doer, Dad shared. I know. I guess that is one of the reasons this is still a conversation that she and I "need" to have George spoke in laughter. "Well son, at least you know that you do not have to think too hard on it, seeing that you are a praying man, I am certain that with HIS help, it will all be worked out" Dad encouraged.

Still Running

Angie was running out of steam and her officemate noticed. Angie, may I ask you a personal question Sarah asked? Sure, and we will see if it is one that I am able to answer. Angie answered with a slight chuckle. How are you feeling, and how are you adjusting to all that you have been through, work and now your blessed new life chapters at home?

Well Sarah, most of the time the way I feel changes by the day, here lately by the hour, but work is good, so for the most part, I feel that I am adjusting pretty good to everything that's happened and going on Angie answered. So tell me, Angie why are you here? Why did you really return to work, and why so soon? With all, that you have been through, the powers that be would have totally understood, had you taken 3 to 6 additional weeks before returning to the workforce. Sarah stated with her question.

Um excuse me, you do know that we are now actually on question number "6" right? Angie responded instead of answering. Nah, I am only giving you a hard time Sarah. Well, let me see. By the way, I cannot believe that I am actually telling you this, but honestly, I am uneasy about being at home, and assuming full time wife and mother duties. I mean to do this all at once, as well as try to figure out a way to fix my extended family, while nursing my own health and well-being too. It is a lot! Wow, did I just say that a loud?

Um, I feel like such a mess, and I am afraid that, the more that I am around my husband the more he will see, the true mess that I am. I cannot be home right now, I just cannot.

I am gonna take this down to the shredder, Angie ended as she left their shared office before Sarah could share her response.

In no hurry to return to the office and face her officemate, or the possibility of returning to the prior, incomplete conversation, Angie bypassed the elevator opting for the stairs, but even in doing this, it did not stop the inevitable, which was a lot sooner than later she would have to return to her workstation. She slowly fed her documents into the shredder and with a sigh headed for the door to return. Before she knew it, she was back on her floor and just a matter of steps from her office. She walked past her office door, continuing on to the restroom. Maybe this would buy her a few additional moments to get her thoughts together and prepare for any additional questions, or uneasy conversations.

Now standing before the sink, she gazed at herself in the mirror as she washed her hands. I guess I need to talk to my husband about my concerns she silently thought. Ump, she sighed as she looked down preparing to walk away from the sink area.

"Hey, surly you are not trying to avoid returning to the office, are you?" Sarah spoke as she playfully bumped into Angie. "Um, yeah," Angie replied with a slight chuckle.

Angie listen, just know, that though few words were spoken just now, a lot was said. Most importantly, just know that the questions were for you. You do not have to answer to me. I am your friend Angie. In no way, do I want to embarrass you, or make you uncomfortable. However, as your friend, I have to be honest in sharing my opinion with you. Girl, I strongly encourage you to share your thoughts and feelings with George; he cannot have the slightest clue that you are fearful about assuming the role of his wife, the homemaker of your home, or as a mother to your precious little one, etc.

For all we know he may be thinking that you do not want to be there with him, or that you have little, to no interest in embracing these roles and more. Just talk to your husband, he's a fare man and he hangs on, to your every spoken word, Sarah spoke with a dramatic flair and laughter. Whatever no he does not, Angie spoke through with parallel laughter. You are so in denial, Sarah spoke but I am going to leave that one alone Mrs. Patient. Come on back in here, we got work to do.

A lot less weighted, Angie was able to return to the office and enjoy a productive workday. Before leaving that day, she wanted to be sure, to once again, thank Sarah. Be it consciously or unconsciously the previously asked question was one she needed to answer. "Um, why did I come back to work, and why now" she silently asked herself? Wow.

I wonder what he is doing right now; she softly spoke while dialing the number. "Hello," George answered. "Well hello to you Mr. Patient, and how is your day going thus far?" Angie spoke. "It's a great day, one that just got better, now that I am getting this call from you. How about you what is the status of your day?" George spoke with an obvious smile. "You know, it had a different and interesting beginning, but even with that, like yours, it's a great day. How is our little one doing?" Angie replied and asked. "Oh he's fine. Right now, we are hanging out with Dad. To be able to watch them two together, is just priceless Angie." George answered. "Awe baby you gotta video as much of that as you can. I hate that I am missing that. I so wish I was there" Angie replied. "Maybe the next time," George replied choosing not to completely say what he was thinking. "I will take pictures and try to get as much footage as I can." "Yeah, please do." Angie requested. "Are you sure that you are okay?" George asked. Yes, love, more than okay. I love you so much George Patient and I am looking forward to coming home to you and our little Mr. Patient this evening.

Hahaha, with talk like that you may have a "full blown fire" already going when you get here. George playfully replied. Is that a promise? Angie abidingly continued in her response. It is now! George answered. Well okay then, it is a date Angie replied sweetly. Hey, tell me what you want for dinner tonight George asked. Sweetie, that is a minor detail, as long as you accompany it. Relax, I trust you whole-heartedly with dinner. Angie answered. "Eewww really you two, hello, I guess no one else is in the room? Oh but wait, it is." Sarah playfully spoke.

Okay, okay I am gonna let you go for now since someone is over here "ear hustling." Angie spoke with laughter as she ended her call, but still offered an apology to Sarah, now that she was off the telephone.

Angie, you owe me no apology for embracing and enjoying your current life chapter. I was only teasing you. Keep cherishing what you have girlie, Sarah encouraged as she grabbed a file on her way out of the office.

Chapter: Two

Checking In On The Koole Family

Family and friends were supportive, but Kathy had been feeling almost defeated, and though she set through countless consultations, it resulted in little, to no confirmed bookings. Was this Kathy, once again wasting the family's money, were titles really going to be her lot? Where were the "confirming call backs?"

A short distance from Kaye's school, Kathy decided to park at the park. Though she refused to voice it, she thought about her disappointment, and how maybe, she should simply give up. She released a soft sigh before collecting her thoughts and readying herself to welcome and receive her daughter at carpool pickup. Placing her disappointment on hold, she donned a genuine warm, confidant smile as she headed to Kaye's school.

More Patience

With it being almost quitting time for both, their wives, George and Dad began to wrap up their outing. Since Dad and Lydia had planes, George took him to the jewelry store instead of home. "Thank you for today Georgie, I love you son." It was my pleasure Dad, thank you! What do you and Lydia have planned George asked? Well she has been looking at a few pieces for the store and she plans to make a decision today Dad answered. Sounds like fun George replied. Yeah son it normally is, you have this ole blind looking man, and innocent young woman enter a well to do, boutique. Naturally, wanting the best possible deal on unique and rare jewelry pieces, you soon learn that everyone's idea of that is not equal. Son, let me tell you, most of the time they are not ready for the knowledge and confidence that she comes with. Watching her in action is like watching the unfolding of a masterpiece. There have been times that it was downright coMiccil son. She has actually walked out without the prized item three times, but twice, she received a call back, and they actually offered the piece on her terms the next day. Yeah she knows her stuff and no matter how long she has been researching and searching, she is not going to be, strong-armed into investing in any jewelry item. Well good for her Dad and she should not be.

Well I love you son, have a good evening. Enjoy your family. Another thing, I hope you are gonna change into a little different attire, the material and the color of that shirt really does nothing for those slack son. It is almost embarrassing. Please be sure to change before your wife gets home this evening. Hahaha, okay Dad, will do George replied. "Until next time grandson. I love you." Dad spoke as he looked back extending his hand to lovingly, greet his grandson before exiting the vehicle.

Now out of the vehicle and just a few steps from the door, George got it. He got it! Wait a minute, hey Dad, wait a minute George spoke as he lowered his window now calling out to his dad. Can you step back over here for a few? Sure, what is it son Dad asked as he returned to the vehicle, now leaning into the window.

Hey Dad, what was that, you were saying about my shirt. You have me a little puzzled Georges confessed. Okay so, a few weeks prior to our wedding day my sight capability changed for the better. Though quite thankful, I did not make a big deal of it at first and I kept the change to myself. With the passing weeks it continue to change for the better so I went to see what the doctor had to say about it. Son, to make a long story short my sight could be restored fully. I am just waiting on the results of some recent tests. The actual level of restoration is the big question for me. That part is yet to be determined, so that is the uneasy part of this   waiting   period.

Well son, if the sight that I have right now, is the best that it will be, it still beats shadows, and grayed or dark spotted of objects any day. To be able to tell Lydia, that she is beautiful both inside and out has new meaning now because I now physically see in a way that I could not at first. Georgie, being able to hold and behold that little one back there was just priceless son, though he's only been here a short while, he has grown and matured so much since I saw him last. I am a richly blessed man son, a richly blessed man.

That's awesome Dad, and right now, I am speechless. I have questions but no idea as to where to start. For now, I choose to rejoice with you, and praise God for restoration of your vision and sight!

Yes, thank you son, God has been and continue to be, so good to me. Let me get inside, Lydia is waiting, I love you guys Dad spoke with the waving of a hand as he backed away from the vehicle to head inside. We love you too Dad, George called out as he pulled off.

Angie had come to the end of her workday. She was more excited, than she had been in a very long time about going home. Sarah shared a lot in there prior conversation, but a few things in particular grabbed Angie's attention. Now she was looking forward to sharing, and talking with her husband this evening. The last thing she would ever want to happen would be for George to silently question, her interest in being his wife and building a home life with him and their son. It was a blessing and honor to be with George and their son. Outside of the, "day to day", task and responsibilities of life, there was no other place that she would rather be. With this, and other encouraging and motivating thoughts to fuel her, that evening, by the end of their conversation, her husband would know and believe this fact, unwaveringly. Again, armed with these thoughts and a warm present smile, and home on her mind, Angie bid those in passing safe travels and a good evening as she left her office heading for the parking lot.

Coming Around

Though Samantha finally embraced the truth of her reality; still yet, she was unable to make any necessary decisions, or even think about any preparation, and don't even mention the talk with Grae which was long overdue. It had been some time since Angie met with them to personally apology; it was time for Samantha to see what Grae was thinking and or feeling about all that had transpired in the passing weeks.

That afternoon Mrs. Aaria left Samantha and Grae alone, giving them the needed time and space for them to talk.

Before leaving carpool that afternoon, Samantha asked Grae if she had any ideas or suggestions for dinner. "Um, no not really," Grae answered. Well do we want to go home and find something to prepare ourselves, decide on somewhere to go, or call in an order for pick up before heading home? Samantha asked. Well, if we have food at home, I say just prepare something at home this time. Grae answered. Okay, there we have it Samantha spoke, home we go.

During dinner preparations, after hearing about Grae's day, Samantha introduced the subject of the recent unfolding in their family. Grae we have had some unexpected and unexplainable things to happen to us as a family, what are your thoughts? I have a bunch of thoughts Grae answered. Will you share them with me? I would like us to think through them together aloud Samantha suggested. If it helps, I am prepared to share some of my thoughts as well. Okay, so you want to talk about it, well you go first, Grae replied in a hasted response. Nice try, but right now our focus is on you and your thoughts, Samantha answered. "But I do not know how to begin," Grae answered. Okay fair enough. Would it help if I began with a few questions to help get you started, Samantha asked? "We can give it a try," Grae answered. Okay but before I began, Grae there is no right and or wrong answer, and I only want your honest and true response. Grae I want you to remember that for you to be honest during this conversation does not mean that you love any of us any less or that you think any less of us. "Okay," Grae offered. Well, should we jump right in or kinda wade in the water a little, Samantha playfully asked? You can just ask me a question Grae answered.

Grae how is all of this for you? All of what, Grae asked? Well to live under the arrangement that we have been living under for all this time, apart from your father and somewhat apart from your mother, Samantha asked. Oh, Grae spoke through a sigh. Well, not living with my father only became uneasy, when I would be teased at school. Outside of that, it really was not something that I thought of. Nevertheless, you always felt like a mother to me, and Aunt Angie has always been Aunt Angie. Since Aunt Angie and Mrs. Aaria was always taking care of you a lot of times you were resting so we did not talk a whole whole lot because I did not want to disturb you. Sweetie you were never a disturbance to me, even though I did not talk a whole lot then, you were always a sweet warm place, and I could always since and feel when you were near, that was comforting for me Samantha shared.

Though silently at first, over the course of time I learned that I have always loved you Grae and it is an awesome thing now, to be able to do that aloud! I know mommy, I love you too Grae replied. Did you have any idea about me being your mother before your Auntie explained everything in her apology? I wondered and had a feeling. Do you remember that day I had to leave school when some of my classmates were saying hurtful

39

things about me. I had never seen you act the way you acted that day at school, and when we came home you were the one that stayed with me the whole evening, we even fell asleep together. You made me feel extra special, and that is when you began to become extra special to me. I am so glad that I get to call you mommy Grae ended. Yes sweetie, I tell you, it truly is an awesome thing.

Now, what about Guy, how do you feel about him? Samantha asked Grae. He is my daddy, and I love him to. How are you able to do that after such a short while, Samantha asked. Well it could be because I did not just meet him a few months ago, that may have a lot to do with it Grae replied. That is right I almost forgot about that part Samantha answered. I do not think I can ever forget that part Grae answered. Isn't it something, when you think about how my friend knew my dad, but she did not know that he was my dad. Then mommy, I actually got the chance to ride in his car when I was with my friend and we did not know who the other was. Mommy, daddy and I were close a few times, we looked right at one another but we did not know. Wow, Grae ended. Sweetie something was different about your eyes when you shared that part Grae, do you get angry, disappointed or upset when you think about how your Auntie's decision separated our family for the last, almost 5 years? Well it is not easy to answer that question because, I love Aunt Angie and I love her all the time, but when I think about it, I do not understand how she could live with us and not tell us who we where to one another. On the other hand, how could she say nothing about my dad living right around the corner almost? To think about that hurts, but just like we were sad, so was she. Just like we were missing something, she was too. So that makes it hard to get angry with her and stay angry because I don't believe she did it because she did not love us, I think she did it because she did love us, even though it doesn't make sense. Mommy it is a lot, but I just know that I am super excited to have a daddy that is super excited about having me back!

Are you kidding me, Grae what about me, why does Guy get "super excited," when you talk about him? Samantha teasingly asked Grae as she showered her with playful pokes and tickles. "Mommy quit it," Grae managed, almost sing between breaths. Okay sweetie, you are right if we plan on, eating anytime soon we need to step into high gear and get the fire started and something cooking.

It had been months, since Angie's letter of confession, as well as her, private verbal apology, to both her sister Samantha and her niece, Grae. Yet Samantha could not bring herself to simply packing her bags and moving her and Grae into the house with Guy.

"God, we both know I do not talk to you as much as I should, I can so understand, if you have to send an Angel, out to the courtyard of Heaven, to see exactly who it is that is seeking your attention. To see who is trying to talk to you right now, but when you get some time, Lord I need you. Please unlock the pockets of my heart and mind, which separate me from the complete truth of my marriage relationship. I need for You, to equip and prepare me to, say, do, respond, and move, accordingly at each appointed time. Please help us, because we need to be honest and right before you, so that our daughter may be spared from any additional hurt pain or suffering, and any possible emotional trauma. God you have been with us, all this time so please do not leave us now, especially since we now know, and understand how much I, we need you. Please help our family, and help me to be comfortable when we share the same space, oh and God it would help if he didn't stare so much to." Thank you God, Samantha concluded with a playful wink directed upwardly. Without any doubt, even with Samantha knowing what her next steps needed to be, it did not change the fact that she was short of the necessary courage to walk them out. Though it may seem minimum to some, right now the continual telephone conversations and periodic meetings would have to do. Samantha had her answer, knew her task but needed more time to embrace the "knowns and unknowns," that came along with moving forward accordingly. Whew, God I thank you in advance for your help.

Work With The Partners

Things were slowing down with the completion of the shelter, and Guy was a little on edge. It appeared that one of his contractors for the project was a little overbooked and it was now affecting the progress of the shelter. Guy had Felicia to touch bases with Janet and Lynn to see if it was possible to squeeze in a meeting that morning once Kevin and Stewart Arrived. She was to get back to him as soon as she had something confirmed. While waiting to hear back from them, Guy did as much of the legwork that he could, making sure all of the necessary information was readily available and on hand when it came time for the meeting.

Now that we are here I just want to cross a few "T's" and dot some "I's" First, well I drove by our two sites and noticed that the shelter is not up to the expected targeted point of progress. Second, the other site for the restaurant looks like, "the end of the day wrap up" is falling off. Some of the equipment left unattended overnight makes me uncomfortable. Let us go back, review their safety procedure, and compare it to our expectations. One of my, rather, our main concern is safety. They all took turns offering their input and collectively devised a list, one they would revisit in a few days, to specifically list out the necessary updates. With this being today's final changes, the meeting was over, and they were all off to their initial tasks of interest prior to this on the spot meeting.

With the pasting of a few days, and the gathering of additional information, Guy, Kevin and Stewart came together for a quick briefing before taking on the workday ahead. Okay first up is the shelter, why are we lagging in the target point of completion? Guy asked.

Well as suspected, "to many seized" opportunities and not enough available working hands on deck, Stewart answered. Okay, so what fall back plan do we have in place for a situation such as this? Guy wondered aloud. I am not sure that we actually have something in writing Stewart continued.

Yeah, I am with Stewart, Kevin added, but aside from it being a family member, Kolin's company is a, one-stop shop for a lot of what we are doing with the shelter and restaurant. If we are interested, we can have them submit over a few specs for a job like ours. We can check some of his clientele, to see what past clients have to say about them and come to a place of decision or we can put some feelers out to see what is out there, or we can take it way back, having the girls make some inquiring calls, maybe get a few quotes and compare offered services.

Okay let us come together two days from now about the same time. I suggest we talk to some of Kolin's clients have the girls' check the specs see if they are interested in a job like ours and get a few comparison quotes from companies that come highly recommended. Again, that is only my suggestion, what do you two suggest, Guy asked. Sounds like a plan to me Stewart answered. Yeah, that is a good starting point; Kevin shared in full support of the suggestion.

Well okay then, if there is nothing more to add, "its back to work fellas," Guy spoke in a bit of an encouraging tone.

Work had been quite helpful in keeping his mind off Samantha, but "if truth be told," it only made Guy's nights a lot longer. Allowing her to choose the timing of their next conversation was not an easy thought or task, but it helped for him to know that whenever she decided to call, she would then, be open and ready to talk to him. This was something he hoped would eventually grant him the access and opportunity to discuss, "them, their family and hopefully a renewed relationship and future together."

He wanted her to believe in him, in them again. Guy wanted her trust and respect, he had no idea of what it would take to win it but he was determined to find out. It was something "he", was ready and willing to be spent for. Though lots of question marks loomed, and after seeing, and believing and knowing it was now possible, one thing was for certain, Guy wanted and needed his family back and he was learning how to fight, the right way to make it happen.

He experienced, both extreme excitement and deep rooted pain after opening, and seeing her on the other side of that door, and to have her to, look at him and walk pass and beyond him as she entered, was even more confirmation that he had no idea of knowing how to gage Samantha's mental and emotional state. Again, Guy thought about how he had been careful in his approach of the re-introduction and the topics of necessary conversation, and often prayed both silently and aloud for God's help in properly addressing and nurturing "them".

"Whew, Lord I thank you for helping me, with receiving and embracing, Your Divine timing and placement".

Life at the office continued to get better and better, both the company, and charity efforts were on track and making upward and forward progress. Most of their clients had pitched in, offering donations, giving of their time, abilities, expertise, and support, and the partners were looking forward to the completion of the projects. Guy, along with the rest of the partners expected and believed total and complete balance would soon be there reality relationally, both professionally and personally.

Daily were the twins maturing and growing, and as much as she could, Grace wanted to capture every moment of it. She was committed and faithful to her sessions and had learned a lot over the course of the passing months. After the birth of her babies, it was scary to think about the path Grace appeared to be heading. With this thought, came a rash and flood of emotions. She envisioned her sweet precious babies, and someone else teaching them how to talk and think while Stewart carried out his workday. It served as a reminded that no level of uneasiness or discomfort was, "too much", if it resulted in her being a better mother for, and to her children. If necessary, she would give her last breath for them. Some time ago, Grace heard that, "the one who teaches your child how to talk in turn teaches them how to think." With this being her added motivation, Grace was equipped and ready for her next and remaining sessions.

Though she still did not have all of the answers, she was ready to be honest, and completely transparent with Stewart. Right now, her truth was that even though she loved him to life and beyond, sometimes he was just too perfect! Apparently, this was something Grace had needed to say to her husband since some time after bringing the twins home. There, she was actually honest enough with herself to complete her thought, and now she was open and willing to tell Stewart. "Wow, though some may say she was being ungrateful, to be able actually tell him, that sometime his "perfectness", simply just irritated her, was a little refreshing. Humph.

Having now arrived at the end of her "self honesty," Grace now considered how uncool it was to feel this way. "Lord, unceasingly and continually, do I need your help. Ump, I won't even ask how or why right now, for my main care and concern, is that you help me to…, I don't know, but You do Lord so you finish the statement, You fill in the blank, and with Your help and by Your grace, I will embrace, receive, move and execute, accordingly!" Well, I guess there will be an addition to the next session, Grace thought out.

So much was weighing down on Stewart that even he could not properly calculate the total effects on him. Of all the time that he and Grace had been together, even going back to when they started talking, and eventually dating, they had never gone this long without truly being able to verbally engage, and connected. In the past Grace had teasingly threatened him to never take away his voice or the intentional, engaging stimulating conversation from her, and he would always jokingly laugh it off by saying "Grace, now who else am I gonna talk to, who would want to listen to the real and complete Stewart Adam?" Well now, as he thought back on that past comment, and some of their past conversations, even if people were, outside lined up at the door, he now knew that he wanted and needed, her conversation, and her voice, just as much, if not more than, she needed and or wanted his. "Ump, talk about taking things, rather people for granted," he softly spoke in a sigh.

Not only was he angry with her for not needing or missing his conversation and voice, but he was angry with her for taking hers away from him.

Guy was out for an appointment so Stewart and Kevin were putting some final touches on an upcoming grand opening. They had very little to review so it was expected to be a rather short meeting.

"Hey, now that that's done, why don't we take a walk up the block and grab something to eat." Kevin suggested assuredly. "Nah, you can go on without me, I am gonna just hang out here for a bit before continuing home. Stewart busily replied. Okay then, maybe another time Kevin offered as he headed for the door. Cool, we will talk tomorrow, Stewart replied as he stacked up files in the motion of sitting down. "Works for me," Kevin spoke.

Now a few feet outside the office door, "no, that is a lie, that doesn't work for me", Kevin added now taking a few steps backward and turning to head back inside of Stewart's office, closing the door behind him. Stewart, there is something that I must honestly, but respectfully share with you.

We all know Guy is a lot better at this but of course, he is not here. Since I am so horrible at stuff like this I am just gonna say it. I believe that you are harboring a little anger for Grace and you have to deal with it. To be honest man, I don't even think you know or see it. I just know, until you do, your family will never see or experience the true healing and restoration necessary for you and your family to go forward. Okay I am sure I have said more than enough. I don't even want you to say anything right now. Because as hard as it was for me to say this, I am guessing, it was a lot harder to hear. I pray that as you think about this, that you will, after hearing the uneasy, that you will be able to make any necessary adjustments. Because your family, whether they know it or not, they are depending on you, they need you and you need them. With a still silence, Stewart sat at his desk during Kevin's short message, able to offer no more than his listening hears. Seeing this Kevin, tried to ease any possible pressure for Stewart to respond by offering a quick, "just know that we love you guys man, and we care, about what happens, and the things that, don't happen to you and for you. Okay, now I can and will leave you to wrap up so you can head home." Kevin spoke and soon after, he was gone.

Guy continued and grew more faithful to his Bible searches and reading.

In recent weeks, he found himself wanting answers about forgiveness. This Search led him to a couple of scriptures however after reading Genesis 45:4-5, he decided to go to the beginning of Joseph's life, to read his story. From the surface, it appeared Joseph had suffered a lot because of one calculated decision by his own flesh and blood, his older brothers. Now Guy would read further and find out what happened and what Joseph eventually did about it.

It had been a few weeks, and after reading all about Joseph, his options and choices, his steadfastness, his level and ability of forgiveness. Guy had a lot to think about. Forgiveness now lingered on his mind even the more. He knew, eventually that he would need to, that he had to, completely let go and forgive Angie, and the role she played in turning his life upside down but he needed help doing this. Though it was something he wanted to do, he had no clue as to how he was going to do it, how he would be able to place it in the past and leave it there. When it came to Samantha and Grae the future was all he saw most days but on the other days Angie was a reminder as to exactly how he and his family had gotten to be in this place.

God how do you do it? Daily you extend mercy and forgiveness to us no matter our fault if only we come to you and humbly apologize, and then we can truly embrace and receive it.

Wow Lord, not that you do not already know this, but this is no small task for me. I hurt daily, and do have days, where I experience more anger than I do on others. I sometimes want her to hurt as I hurt. I sometimes want her to feel this deep, rooted pain and loneliness too. I know none of this is right but I must tell you the truth. Although what I see at times can throw me off, I choose to thank you in advance for proper peace and balance, both professionally and personally.

It seemed like it had only been a matter of weeks, since Stewart had shared the importance of a song with the fellas. He reminded them that, "when", they found themselves not, in the very best of space, at home with their wives, or in their marriage, that sometimes lyrics could speak to you when no one else could or would.

Now it was his turn, to reach back for that reminder. Though he would not actually tell anyone, lately Stewart had been charting through, "day to day life on E, with no reserves". Mentally and emotionally, he was depleted, he had nothing left; he was completely "Empty!" Though it helped, to know, to understand and believe, that "this too shall pass, and that joy comes in the morning", Stewart, wasn't certain he could hold on until another morning, or for that moment of joy, too much longer, not knowing exactly when that would be. He wanted to feel and see a difference now?" Where was the "passing," on into the joy? He needed it now.

Right now, his beautiful children were his, "why", but how long would he be able to live life on that wave of adrenalin? He missed his cheerleader, his biggest supporter and number one fan. He desperately needed his life mate and best friends' conversation. He missed her voice and input, on, about the big things, and the little things, in the big situations as well as in the small. Even in his, "silly thought" moments. Stewart needed

Grace in many ways, for just as he was for her, he too was truly, "all things Grace."

God please help us, help me to stand still and hold on. Help me, to be the man the husband and father that I need to be in this season. Help me to always honor and please You, no matter what goes on in or around my life. JESUS, we need your continual covering and comfort right now because right now, our flesh is weak, and the attitude of stubbornness and selfish fleshliness, is trying to park in our home, relationship, and life. We need you to block it and remove it God replacing it with more of, "You, your God-nature, and attributes".

Today Stewart found himself needing a song. This took him on a journey in his mind to when he saw Grace for the first time. He had gone to Ohio for a youth convention. Even though the hotel lobby was crowded with people waiting on their turn to check in, Stewart managed to notice a beautiful young girl passing through the lobby area on her way out. Much later after arriving at the convention, he saw the same young girl again, only this time, she did not disappear as fast as before, but to him it was still too soon to see her go. A day later, she stood just a matter of steps behind him as he gathered his breakfast items. It was then he decided he would talk to her if nothing more than, hello. He had to say something to her but how would he say it? While he wrestled with his dialect and the delivery of his "hello", a bold and confident young man walked up initiating conversation with her. When young Steward turned around, and ready to make his move all he could manage was "excuse me" as he reached across her while she continued in her conversation. Even though he walked, upright and tall, across the room to accompany the rest of his group, inside he felt shrunken. Even back then, a song came rushing to mind. ♪ ♪ "Can we talk for a minute, girl I want to know your name…"

More than two days had passed and still, Stewart failed at, actually talking to this beautiful young woman. Time was moving fast, and the convention was soon to end. He considered writing her a quick letter, but what would he write, how do you introduce yourself to a stranger in a note? Finally, he had the proper thought, "God I would like to meet this young lady and if you agree, please work it out." In the following days, before all the young people where completely packed, loaded, and set to drive off to their many different destinations, HE did just that, HE worked it out perfectly. That last morning, bright and early, at breakfast she sat at a table alone. Quick to seize the moment of answered prayer, he humbly approached her table leading with a simple greeting. "Good morning, I am Stewart Adam, may I join you?"

From that moment on, their connection grew stronger with each conversation, and there were many before the two would actually see each other again.

This short trip of "remembering when," warmed Stewart's heart in a way in which he, here lately, had forgotten was possible when it came to thoughts of his wife. Lord, if I have been selfish or judgmental in any way please forgive me. Thank you for allowing me to see me, and for helping me to be, "who and what" you desire for me to be in this hour, in this season of our marriage and life. Um, "In good times and in bad, in sickness and in health...I Do."

However, not always easy, I said it, and I meant it Lord. I still mean it today. Your word reminds us that, "when we are weak, You are strong," and God, right now, I sure need your strength. I am desperately, in need of Your strength. Eventually, a soft warm smile painted his face as he located and played his first "Grace" song, one of the songs that took him back to the memory of their meeting, "Can we talk for a minute, girl I want to know your name…"

Remembering When, Remembering Why

Stewart, was beginning to see, how over the last few months, he had managed to close the door on "some things Grace." It was a coping mechanism, he had learned to expect less and less from and of her. Once he became "non-expectant," as it related to Grace and her daily input, it appeared to help him make it through the day, enabling him to do everything he could possibly do, and then some, "solo" almost as if he was a single parent."

Thinking about it now, he felt conviction, and realized in a way, he too had checked out. Stewart had become pretty good at checking out of the areas that were more challenging for him to deal with at home. It was unfair to Grace, the children and him. Though the farthest thing from the truth, and be it consciously or unconsciously, Stewart was sending the message that neither he, nor the children, needed Grace. It was a message that Grace was very conscious of, and now so was he.

Well God, here I am once again, needing even more "damage control" assistance. "Man, its recovery time. It is time for us to win at life again, it is time for us to claim it, and walk in victory! Help us win God, help me do, whatever I need to do that "I, Me, and My," may be replaced by, "You;" we, and us". I invite and welcome You in. Move me out of the way that Your will and hand may come in, and once again totally rule, and reign, in and upon our relationships and life.

Lord, we want all of your best, in every way shape form and fashion, this is what we seek and want in and upon our life. Even if, it means that we must be uncomfortable for a moment to get there. I just know that we have been here for a while now and this is not a healthy place. This is not the place for us to be and we choose to move on and graduate from this trial. I believe that with your help we can and will do just that. Ump, we have to God, we just have to!

Dealing with loneliness was one thing, but this type of emotional imbalance was taking a toll. He had yet to decide which was worse, "silently going through the motions of life with question marks, in secret and alone, or with full knowledge, as an open book before God and his friends?" Either way, until he properly addressed it and dealt with it, it was something he had very little to no control over.

Some days, hearing her name, or just the thought of it made him angry, but if having his family was his true desire and focus, not only would he have to get use to embracing Angie's name, but her face and presence as well. "Wow God I gotta be honest, in my mind I do sometimes wonder how this will be possible, but I won't park there, I will pray instead. One of my continual prayers is that you will help me, to totally, and completely forgive, to forgive myself as well as Angie. I choose to extend and receive self-forgiveness, and I choose to extend total forgiveness to Angie. Help me Lord, to release the bad, the anger and past faults, faults of my own as well as the faults of others, that I may embrace the future you have in store for me, and my family. Help me to be, to do and say what it takes that I may be properly positioned to be blessed by You, to receive the fullness of Your promises in and upon my life, our life."

Still lingering in his prayer thought, and the reality of some of his necessary adjustments, Guy was a little less than excited by an incoming telephone call.

Guy speaking, he answered. Hey Guy, its Stewart do you have a few minutes, I want to run a few things by you. "Sure, why not" Guy replied through a sigh. Wait a minute; you sound a little bothered buddy, what is eating at you? Stewart asked.

"Wow, interesting choice of words my friend, interesting choice of words." Guy replied. Well I take that as my confirmation then. Therefore, again I will ask, "What's eating at you?" Stewart asked his friend in an attempt to encourage him to deal with it, whatever his "it," was. I Tell you what Stewart, I am not sure where you are right about now but if I see you within the next 10 minutes or so, you are sure to get more than an ear full, Guy replied. Okay, I except that challenge Stewart answered, one thing though, make that 20 minutes and it is a confirmed appointment. Okay, the appointment is set Guy answered. Okay, then off the telephone we go, Stewart replied, I have an appointment to keep. Wait, you said that you wanted to run a few things buy me, Guy reminded. Oh that was just business, it can wait right now a friend is counting on me. Gotta go, he replied and ended the call.

Now that Stewart was present, front and center Guy, in detail answered his prior question. Once, he had revealed that which was on his heart and his current thoughts and feelings of and toward Angie, Stewart asked Guy some questions.

Okay Guy first I need to remind you, "don't shoot the messenger." Well, wait a minute, now I have one for you, "if looks could kill", oh is that a threat, Stewart asked with a chuckle. Of course not, Guy answer with a quick soft smile, just the first thing to my mind. Go ahead, what is it that you want to ask me?

"Have you been thinking more and more about your family Stewart asked? Yeah, I know that it may not be possible, but it feels like every moment of the day, Guy answered. Tell me something, are you more angry with Angie because she played a major role in keeping you from your wife and eventually your family when she sent you a letter supposedly on behalf of your wife, or at you for being so passive, for so long and not fighting harder for your wife and family?" Guy spoke no words, for a few moments the best that he could offer was direct eye contact. "Wow, I am glad that they don't", Stewart spoke respectfully. What did you just say? Guy asked. "I said that I am glad that they don't," Stewart spoke again. I was just going back to when you said, "If looks could kill." Oh, so you think you saw one of those looks? Guy asked with a snicker. Yes sir, or at least one of the closest things that I have seen to it Stewart replied.

You know what Stewart I do not think that I have ever, been more floored by you then right now. I mean, I still do not know how to take the question, let alone how to answer it. Wow, forget about calling the game over, you shut down the entire park with that question Guy replied.

Okay, fare enough, Stewart responded. Let us just shelf it for later, better yet, your answer does not have to include me, it is all for you. Take it as, simply a question to get to a true and complete answer, what we are looking for here is the root of why you think and or feel what you do. In no way am I questioning the, "who, and or what", that you are. This is not a question, "of, who or what you were," at that time this all began either. Please, do not even entertain that thought at all. We just want to make sure you are in a place where even if you never ever forget this whole ordeal, that you will be able to totally, completely, and truly let go of the blame hurt, pain, disappointment, and any possible bitterness you may have felt or are feeling. We want closure of this painful life event. Because when you get your family back, and you will get them back, you also get Angie back. Other than Samantha, she is all Grae knows so you cannot expect her to go away and disappear but most importantly, you cannot want her to. You have to decide in your mind that she is welcomed, and once you are convinced everyone around you will be convinced.

Stewart, I am so floored right now that I do not know if I should be trying to ask you questions or responding from my point of view, Guy finally spoke. Well, I am open to either my friend. I mean, we are talking about, your life. Please, I invite you to say what you feel needs to be said and heard. You know what Stewart, for the first time in a long time, with all of the things that are in plain view, and at the forefront of my minds-eye, I open my mouth to speak and not one of those things are spoken. Can you believe it? I am not sure, if it is because of, not knowing what to say, or because I have so much that I could say but I guess I am speechless. Um, looks like I am going to have to shelf this one for a bit. Even though we have this crazy awkwardness in the air, I guess I should say thank you. If for nothing more than simply showing up, thank you Stewart, you have given me a little yet a lot, the simple and yet the complex to think about. Whew. Hahaha, on that note I am going to just head out Stewart replied. You are welcome. He spoke as he left.

Guy Gets Down To The Core

It had been a few weeks and though work was moving along fine, Guy still had no answer to Stewart's question, or did he? Taking a pause from a file he had opened before him, he gave Stewart a quick call. "Hey Stewart, are you consumed with anything pressing right now?" Ump, well I would not say that, Stewart replied. Though I am busy, you know that I am never too busy for you buddy, what is up? Okay, that is all I needed to know Guy spoke and quickly ended the call. Okay then, Stewart spoke as he returned the phone. Before he could refocus his attention, Guy was stepping inside Stewart's office closing the door behind him. "Okay, what were you really saying to me with the question you asked me? Guy asked. No, no, no, wait a minute, Stewart replied. It is not that I was "saying", per say. It truly was a question. Sometimes we miss the opportunities to give ourselves the self-check that we need. Okay, this has nothing to do with me, but just a few weeks ago, I found myself in the same position. Can you believe that, Kevin was all over it? He was the one instrumental in getting me to a place where I could get outside of myself, and focus upon what I have with Grace, "or the lack there of" right now.

You know what I found, well just as Grace had taken or was withholding from me, I began to do the same. When the thing that you say you want, is in jeopardy, sometimes, you have to, "say; do, be, and or give," as you always did, if not beyond, to safeguard, and shelter what you have. To secure what you have and to keep it from being swept away from under your feet right before your eyes as you sit or stand by watching it drift away all the while as you are being selfishly justified to do nothing or not do the extra "…", fill in the blank.

With a sigh and real deep breath, Guy softly spoke, "I guess she did what she thought she had to do at that moment." Ump at that time, I was focused on laying the foundation for the company, on creating a brand and name. That is mostly what I saw. The funny thing is I have always known that Samantha has never needed me. Her strength is one of the things that captivated my heart, yet one of the things that terrorized me the most, and she always had everything under control. Even when she didn't, Samantha remained so calm cool and level headed that I never knew anything other than this to be true. Unless she actually said so, I was ignorant to that fact. In so many ways, Samantha became my strength, and you know, I have never had a supporter and encourager like Samantha. Ump Stewart, she was supposed to always be there. "Life," for life Stewart, she was supposed to be there for life, then one day she pulls a disappearing act while I was out of town and she… ump, she did it with a letter. Guy I hear you but I also hear you pointing fingers still, except this time they are being pointed at your wife. Nevertheless, as for the letter, let us just say, for the sake of saying, that it was her sister's idea, better yet, that the letter never came from Samantha. I mean, I realize this line of thinking is a little late now, being that Angie has since confessed that she sent the letter on Samantha's behalf and that Samantha never even knew about a letter. However, if we could go back to the time, to the time before we were, armed with this knowledge, how was it so easily accepted that your wife could or would have written you a letter like that?

Come on Guy, the original question is still on the table, but let me remind you the answer is more so for you then a listening audience. First, I was speechless, then mentally and psychologically weak, which was later followed by anger and sealed with pride. This caused me to be numb and I ignored and or avoid all that I could outside of work. Next thing I knew it was four, close to five years later and you loaded me in a vehicle, took me for a ride and asked me some questions right when I was out in the deep about to sink. I knew I needed to wake up. I knew I needed to do something. I knew I needed to face and address some things, but … Wait a minute Guy, Stewart interrupted. Are you sure this conversation is okay for now? No, it is long overdue, Guy answered. I felt like I was on the outside looking in with the key in my hand not knowing how to get inside; having the tool not knowing how or when to use it. Waiting for the moment when I felt that I deserved to be both in possession of the key and actually use it. I left her, in a sense I walked out on her and I did not deserve a second chance.

Which is probably one of the reasons, I did not understand your relationship and comment to God, you see I strongly believe you and Grace deserved His blessings and goodness, but I knew that I did not. It was me, and not Angie. Even though it was not the right thing to do, at least she did something to protect someone she loved. When I got on a plane with my wife and child in a medical crisis, she acted upon her concerns for her sister's well being.

Um, who does that Stewart, what loving husband does that. Where was the care, where was my heart, where was the love? I chose work. I chose work. I disappeared behind work, believing Samantha was good, and like always, that she had it until I got back; it was only going to be for a few days.

Stewart not only had I never seen weakness from Samantha, but she was so confident in who and what she was that she managed to always know exactly how to let me lead as the man, the king of our little castle, Guy spoke with a humble chuckle. I always admired the way she balance being strong, vocal and very present and she did so in and with proper submission all at the same time. Some may doubt that is possible, but I have seen it, and I have; well, we have lived it. She had a way of respectfully, handling me with "man-baby" gloves at the same time. Man, she so spoiled me Stewart, Guy ended with a sigh. Samantha truly is my once in a lifetime find.

You know, Angie was not excited about my relationship, and later marriage to her sister Samantha, maybe now I can somewhat see why that was. You all really need each other. Listen Guy, none of this was about pointing out your faults, but more importantly, for your necessary preparation to reunite you with your family. Guy, don't you dare fret my friend you are doing a lot better than you can see right now, and I honestly believe that you are so much closer to your new beginning with your family then you probably dreamed. Keep being honest and open to the truth, and the role that you played or did not play and your resolve will be at hand quicker than the dawning of the new day. Stewart encouragingly shared.

Grace To Share

Time seemed to move along quickly and today was the day, Stewart would accompany Grace at her appointment and surprisingly, she was a little anxious to have him present. When Grace entered the building, Stewart was already their awaiting her arrival.

"Well, look at you!" Stewart spoke as Grace entered. "Hey Love, now why am I, not surprised, that you beat me here today?" She asked with a giggle. A few minutes later and it was appointment time and they vanished behind closed doors.

Delanda McNair

Chapter – Three

Angie Goes Home Truly For The First Time

Now turning into the driveway, from within, Angie smiled even the more. After parking, she lingered a few moments longer as she gathered her things. "Lord I thank you, this new life is so far different from what I truly deserve. Thank you God, help me to, openly show gratitude and appreciation to and for those that you see fit to bless me with by placing them in my life.

When Angie entered, George had the table, set and the only thing missing was the food on the plate and his family gathered for dinner. "Hey family, smells like somebody lives here!" Angie playfully spoke as she entered. Good because we have been working hard this evening George replied with, outstretched arms as he greeted his wife with a warm embrace. Angie welcomed, and matched her husband's hug then moved to her son resting in a lounge basket on the countertop. Well, just say the word and when you are ready, we can eat. George advised. After hearing this, Angie kissed her son, excused herself, and quickly returned and family time was officially in play.

It was a great evening, the food was wonderful, the conversation was better than, "old times" and George and Angie both looked forward to more evenings similar to this one.

It had been some time since Guy and Samantha had spent that very precious yet unexpected evening together and since it was a great evening why was Samantha so little on time for him or his conversation. Guy did not understand and this had Guy a little bothered but he would have to shelf these thoughts and move on with his workday. A few more days had passed, the partners came together to collaborate on how and what they were going to do to move forward and were able to get most of the updates implemented and activated almost instantly.

Now, with a clearer "headspace" about work, Guy had left all the messages that he wanted to and was all geared up to take a different approach. The first stop was home to shower off the workweek, and his second stop would be an unplanned visit to see Samantha and Grae. Samantha was out when Guy arrived so he offered to relieve Ms. Aaria to get an early start on her weekend. "No, I will just go wrap up a few things while you two catch up." Ms. Aaria politely declined. With a chuckle Guy responded, "I truly understand, and I appreciate your nice, "no, it is not gonna happen" response. I tell you what, hold tight, do not move, you stay right there Guy spoke on as he pulled out his cell phone "Hey, Samantha where are you? " Excuse me?" Samantha replied, clearly heard over the speaker. "Okay, you are right. Guy answered. Right now that's technically none of my business." Ump, yeah, that's what I'm saying." Samantha replied. "Wait a minute, hey sweetie she greeted her daughter before requesting that Guy, take her off speaker" after catching Grae's snickers. "Hey" Grae and Guy responded almost in unison as he took the call off speaker. Really Guy, stop stealing my babe's greeting, I was talking to Grae. "Oh, well excuse me then madam; just be stingy why don't you." Guy spoke sassily but jokingly.

"What are you calling me about", Samantha asked, now with warm, gentle laughter. So what is up Guy? I want to hang out with Grae and when I offered to relieve Ms. Aaria, she would not budge. Guy spoke as he looked at Ms. Aaria bringing her into the conversation. Let me speak with Ms. Aaria Samantha requested. After making sure Grae had completed her evening chores, she got Grae on the line reminding her how a little, "young lady in the making," is to act and conduct herself then, Samantha was back on the line with Guy. Well Mrs. President, do I have clearance   to   leave the compound this evening, I promise to check in to let you know our whereabouts so we can later collaborate on the return time once you wrap up what you have going on. Are you cool with that, "Ms. Excuse Me?" Guy asked with a chuckle. You know what "Mr. Smarty," ump…Samantha began in her response as she allowed a little awkward silence to fill the air…"No not until you tell me", Guy could not pass up feeling that silent moment by answering the rhetorical question. Actually, that works out fine. Samantha answered. Okay we will be in touch later on Guy offered in closing. Okay Samantha responded as they ended the call.

So where are we going, and what are we going to do "Ole Little Beautiful One"? Guy asked Grae. Ump, that is a good question daddy, ump, let me think she answered. What did you say? Guy asked Grae. "Ump, good question, let me think?" Nope! Guy answered. It is, Grae replied. No, it is not Guy somewhat sang in his response. Well, what did I say? Grae asked. What you actually said: "Ump, that's a good question daddy… "Ump, let me think", Guy answered. "Daddy" Grae managed to speak over her giggle. If you heard me the first time why did you ask what, did I say? Well can you keep a secret Guy Asked? Well it depends, Grae answered, sometimes keeping secrets is a bad thing, Daddy. Sometimes, some things need to be told. Okay, totally understand your point Beautiful. I will just tell you anyway. Guy answered. Okay, Grae replied. "Wutcha got?"

It makes me happy to be able to hear you call me Daddy. Though little to some, five years is a lot of life Honey. That is, one thousand eight hundred and twenty five days of life, in which I was not a part of. It was time lived separately from you and your mom, and it is still a big deal to me. I can talk to you, I can see you, I can spend time with you, it is all a big deal Grae, and a great blessing. Instead of a verbal response Grae extended her little arms to embrace her Daddy, and seeing where she was headed Guy lowered down to his knee to welcome and receive her hug.

Okay Daddy I got it, Grae spoke with excitement, okay wutcha got, Guy asked. I know where we are going and what we are going to do. Grae answered. Okay, do you care to share the details Guy asked. Sure Grae answered. Come on, we can talk as we walk. Grae added as she sweetly directed her daddy to the door.

Now with their being no reason for Samantha to rush home what was she going to do with the rest of her evening. If Grae could have it her way, she would never leave her daddy's side. Ump, God is this you or is it me, telling us to move into the house with Guy? Yes, I got married to be married and not live separately but even if I go back to the house, we could still be living separately. I know that Grae is in love but after all this time, I am not sure that I am. With the way we ended up here, at this point and time does it even matter? I mean what is my assurance to being in love or does that part, not really matter. I don't know, God, I mean I like him, and he is cute and all but, "So! So what, that he is cute? Wait a minute, who am I kidding? He's way more than cute, but cute doesn't make a marriage, or a relationship work."

Samantha spent the rest of her short drive thinking and talking to God. When her vehicle came to a stop, Samantha found herself parked outside of Mr. Sandosjuah's store. It was closing time but seeing who it was he was more than happy to close a little later than usual. He continued to tidy a few things as he awaited her entry. When that took longer than he felt, he stopped what he was doing to lift his head to see what was taking her so long, but only to see Samantha still seated in the car in her seat belt. Finding this a little odd Mr. Sandosjuah headed to the door, continuing outside to Samantha's car. "Hey young one, do I have to crawl inside or are you going to get out of this car?" He spoke as he softly knocked on the window. Thanks to the wave of distracting thoughts, Samantha's response was delayed so he thought he should knock again, but just as he raised his hand to do so Samantha looked up and released a startling scream. "Oh no, I am so sorry my dear" Mr. Sandosjuah spoke. I had no intention of scaring you, please forgive me. Slowly but softly smiling Samantha finally released her seat belt as she removed her hand from her chest close to her heart. Come on inside and you can yell at me over tea or coffee, Mr. Sandosjuah offered with a chuckle. Now more relaxed and wearing a full smile Samantha got out of the car reaching to hug Mr. Sandosjuah. "No way, I don't ever want to yell at you Mr. Sandosjuah. We are friends, more than that, I consider you as family! Nevertheless, yes, let us get inside. Tell me, what are we going to eat with the tea or coffee? Samantha asked. Well, that is a good question young one, we will have to conduct a quick survey and answer that question once we get inside he answered. Okay, fare enough Samantha responded.

Once inside they put together a meal, and into the oven, it went. Now that the water was hot, they enjoyed great conversation and a good cup of tea as part of the meal cooked. They talked about things going on at the shop and Samantha shared the different things currently on her mind. Her thoughts were somewhat split between things years and months ago and things, in and of her now. She began with the delivery, the delivery that lead her to that "oh so familiar," house. Mr. Sandjosuah listened a lot and offered, many words of wisdom which Samantha desperately needed, and the timing of this visit proved to be, perfect. By the end of the evening though a little uneasy, Samantha was confident and sure of what her next step would be. Thinking back over the time just spent with Mr. Sandosjuah and how he seemed to have an explanation and answer for everything she was concerned with and needed to talk about, moved Samantha to tears as she drove off. She was so grateful and felt extremely blessed to have him as a friend. "Wow, thank you God, look at you! You know exactly what you are doing, don't you?" Well duh, of course You do. Be it quietly hidden, in plain view, or presented openly, right before one's eyes, ump.

Once again, Samantha was in route to somewhere, but with no particular destination in sight. This time her drive led her down a stretch of road with cascading trees, so much so that neighboring treetops almost met, and branches spilt over almost like waterfalls as if they were reaching and stretching for the treetops across the street.

Samantha picked up her phone, but soon placed it back. "What's the point, I am here now." She spoke aloud, now turning into the driveway, which answered her prior unspoken question. So now that she saw that this is where, "the where" was, now what? God this is awkward, it is a lot easier when he is not here. Are you sure that this is where I am supposed to be right now? Quietly Samantha sat in her car now parked in the driveway, unmoved she hesitated on releasing her seatbelt maybe in the hopes of another assigned destination and trying to give God the chance to change His mind and release her from this step she was now, expected to take. Just as she was about to confirm in her mind that she just needed to start the car and get back on the same road that had brought her here there was a soft knock on her window, introducing waves of excitement and a big smile. "Mommie, we are glad you decided to come over. Come on, get out of the car!"

Samantha looked over to see her radiant daughter, bursting with joy. A few steps behind Grae Guy stood, with a soft smile and nod of the head inviting Samantha to come on inside, and that's exactly what Samantha did. Guy led the way and Grae pulled up the rear with her mother in tow. For the first time since her birth, they were together. To be here and have both of her parents there together was absolutely, priceless.

Once inside Grae loaded one of the movies she and her dad picked up earlier. Once her dad took a seat she grabbed her throw and curled up beside him. With his heart being so warm inside that it could melt, Guy softly rested his arm over his daughter's shoulder planting a loving kiss at the top of her forehead.

Still a little challenged by the feeling of not being in control, Samantha watched them from a short distance from across the room as she surfaced from the bathroom. When Guy noticed she had returned, he lifted his free arm inviting Samantha to sit on the other side of him. Samantha politely smiled as she headed toward Grae to have a seat. Trying not to show his disappointment Guy relaxed his free arm, giving more attention to the movie.

When Samantha crossed before him to have a seat next to him, under his arm Guy released a special sigh as everything about him smiled being able to spend an evening such as this with two of his most favorite girls in the world, his wife and his daughter. Surely, this was one of his better moments. One that he wished, he could freeze in time, even if it was for a few moments. Soon after the excitement of all being together in one place, instead of them watching the movie, the movie, in turn was watching them.

About an hour or so later, movement and sighs from Grae woke both Samantha and Guy. "Is she okay", Guy asked. "Ump, that's bathroom movement", Samantha answered. "I don't know if I should offer or not, but I can take her if you want. Guy responded. "No, that's okay; this little missy will be walking herself to the bathroom." Samantha replied as she once again crossed over Guy to get Grae to the bathroom. When Samantha returned, she returned minus Grae. Hey, Guy, I just put Grae to bed in the bedroom at the end of the hall. Is that okay?

"Sure, you gave her one of the best rooms in the house," he replied releasing a yawn. Really, how did it earn that status Samantha asked? Well, outside of it housing the biggest and best sleeping bed in the house, it use to be, well technically "still is" ours. Guy spoke, passing Samantha now on his way to the bathroom himself.

Silently Samantha walked back to the end of the hallway looking in on Grae and taking in the room. Now out of the bathroom, Guy pointed Samantha in the direction of their closet with her clothes still in tack as she had left them years ago. "Why don't you find something comfortable to change into and crawl in bed with Grae?" Guy spoke, while grabbing comfortable clothing himself. Having located what he wanted, he grabbed a blanket and pillow on his way out, closing the bedroom door behind him.

For a few moments, Samantha stood there contemplating on what to grab, her keys to head home, or comfortable clothing as suggested. However, as she looked back at Grae, she was almost jealous as to how comfortable and peaceful she looked to be resting. "Okay Samantha, this is Grae's dad, your husband, just relax, get comfortable and get some well needed rest and sleep." She reminded herself as she walked deeper into the closet, to find something that she could sleep in, then tossing it on the bed on her way out. "Hey Guy." She called out to announce her coming down the hall. "Yeah?" he called back. "Do you have an extra tooth brush, I know Grae has her little overnight kit but I do not." Sure, give me a second I will get it. Guy replied getting up to meet Samantha in the hallway, here you go mostly everything that you will need, will be found in either of these two closets.

"Have a good night," Guy offered as he heads back down the hallway away from Samantha.

Off to the bathroom Samantha went and eventually on to bed. As soon as Guy made it back to his blanket and pillow, he was out like a light. It was a different story for Samantha, this time things were different, sometime ago she felt she knew what she was supposed to do sleep, where she belonged and where both she and Grae should be. Laying in bed, wide-awake, and staring at the ceiling, her mind was completely unlocked. Right now, it was clear, as clear as it was that day Guy almost ran into her at that intersection. As clear as, the second time, she had laid eyes on him and decided that he was one of her least favorite people. As clear as it was, when he just would not go away and their paths continued to cross, and eventually intertwine. As clear as it was, that night she was stuck with him as a game partner, and they chose to mime to a song, in which she was shocked that he actually knew. Moreover, as clear as it was the day he shared his business plan with her, and asked her to be both, his business, and life partner, and that he meant, and expected it to be for life.

So much emotion came over her that her body trembled, as she silently cried. Finally, she slid out of bed, and left the room, to keep from disturbing Grae. Slowly, she gently walked down the hallway, bypassing Guy and on into the rest of the house she took a tour of their home like never before. Her self-guided tour, eventually lead her to the basement. It was here that she wept the most, remembering how she won the rights to decide the use of it many years ago. One round of rock paper scissor with Guy and the choice was hers. Everything was exactly as she had left it. For the last time she left that basement, her life changed, but you could not tell by looking in this room. Who would have thought that her trip to the hospital would have had such a turnout? Being rushed to the hospital that day, for Samantha, began, as a simple trip, that later, prove to have a much unexpected conclusion.

By now, Guy was up and moving, he was heading to the bedroom to look in on Samantha and Grae, but hearing movement from a different area of the house cause a redirecting of his attention. He moved toward the source of the noise to investigate. Seems the more he walked the more the noise and movement stirred. As he got closer to the basement, he noticed the opened door and the light, once he was closer enough to be able to see down the steps, he saw Samantha seated at the bottom of the steps looking through their "Dream Saturday" magazine. She now knew, why that house she stood in, the day of Mrs. Lumma's delivery had the effect that it did. She and her husband had handpicked the house. Outside, from the mortar, brick and roof, to the entrance door, lighting, color scheme, flooring, window treatment, walls appliances, and flooring. It was something they took pleasure in doing, room by room. She and Guy had literally handpicked that house from the inside out, down to the grass and landscape, long, long ago.

Hearing her cry, Guy was not sure if he should go to her or allow her, space. When Samantha stood, turning to head up the stairs, it put to rest, his moment of indecision. Immobilized he stood there at the top of the stairs looking down toward her. Once their eyes met Samantha held up the Magazine, with tears streaming down her face, "I've stood in this house, Guy I've been in this house before, is it still yours?" Samantha asked. No, Guy answered. "Why Samantha?" asked sobering, "why?" Baby, as it always was, it is ours! I could not bring myself to sale it and believe me; I have turned down a whole lot of offers. Moreover, a few, radically ridicules offers might I add, but that house is not about the money, it is so much more to it than that.

Samantha, you were the only girl that heard what I was saying both, when I spoke, and spoke not. There were moments when you had a better understanding of my thoughts and little wisdom then I did. My dreams became like poetry in motion with you, they came true, and from the day I returned to town, having left you her in the hospital a few days prior, I stopped dreaming. I went from dreamer to sleeper, and I have been sleepwalking through life for a long time now.

Guy, I am so torn right now that I do not know what to say. However, I know what to do, just not what to say, Samantha spoke. What do you mean? Guy asked. Guy I love my sister, I do not know how life would be without her, but my sister, Angie played a major role in our separate living. It hurt both you and me, and it stole a lot from Grae. It hurt us all, even Angie herself. I am aware that you may not sympathize with that or the possibility of that reality right now but it is true.

I know that Grae and I belong where you are. We have to sort through these pieces and mend our family, it is past time for us to come together as a family, but I need you to know and understand that you agreeing to this means, you agreeing to welcoming and embracing Angie, my sister, as well. She is my, our family. Grae and I cannot shut Angie out when we return home to you. Know that, wanting and receiving Grae and I, is you wanting and receiving Angie as well. So take some time to think about all of that, but just know, that as you think about it, that whatever you come up with, that Grae and I are coming home. Samantha spoke, now standing next to him and resting her hand on his shoulder.

As Guy took a breath to speak, wait a minute Samantha spoke. Whatever you may be thinking, hold those thoughts. I want to check in on Grae. So silently, Guy stood there, as he watched her walk away toward the bedroom as he continued in his silent talk to God.

"Wow, I guess you both, told and showed me Lord. Ump, I do not know "the how or the when," but with your help, we will do this. *This* will happen God; with your help, we will do this. Not only are we worth this and so much more, we are all in need of it. "Redemption, Forgiveness and Restoration", is what we need God. I know that I do not totally understand Your Word but it reads, "Love covers a multitude of sin…" and "that You will restore the years…" Help me to love the way that I need to, so that we, that I can grow and move past and beyond this fault. I choose to look to our expected future, instead of focusing on the lost years, and the separation from my family. Lord, thank you in advance, for restoring the years, I believe just as you did for those in bible days so it can and will be done here and now. Just as You restored Joseph and his people in the book of Exodus, and David in the book of Psalm, please do it for us. I now know that forgiveness and love is a big thing, and daily, do I need Your help in extending and receiving it. Ump."

Okay ladies, brush your teeth, get the crust out of the corners of your eyes, and throw on some clothes! This train leaves the station in twenty minutes. Guy spoke walking in the direction of Samantha and Grae with an elevated voice.

Good morning mommy, are we going on a train ride? Grae managed to ask, wrapped in a stretch and yawn. Good question Grae, one for which I do not have an answer. I guess the best way for us both to find out is to do what the man says. Samantha teasingly spoke as she softly poked at Grae.

Now outside and leaning against the nose of the vehicle, Guy waited for Samantha and Grae to accompany him. He got the girls loaded and headed for the driver seat. "Okay, here's your drink." He informed Samantha as he extended a mug to her. "Grae, you have a choice of Apple or Orange juice back there, daddy couldn't remember which one is your absolute favorite so I grabbed both to make sure I had you covered." Guy spoke, sealing it with a wink.

"Awe, thank you," Samantha interjected. "Thank you daddy," Grae responded. Are we really going on a train ride? Ump, not today beautiful, that was just a figure of speech, but it does not mean that we cannot do that one day. Guy answered. So where are we going Samantha asked. Hold that thought he answered. Besides, I can show you a lot better than I can tell you, Guy ended with a smile. With that being said; they were now in motion and headed to their destination to see firsthand what Guy had in store.

Is anybody hungry? Guy asked. I am Grae answered. So what would you like, are we wanting a "plate" type situation, or a quick breakfast sandwich? Guy asked. "Well that depends, Grace spoke, and is breakfast the main station for this train" Grae asked with a chuckle. Nope, but we will make time for food. Guy replied with laughter. Okay, I suggest a quick breakfast sandwich, and then we can do the "plate" situation once we leave the main station. Grae giggled as she answered.

So, mommy what do you say? Grae asked. Yeah, what do you say mommy, Guy repeated flirtatiously. I am with Grae, Samantha answered. Let us grab a quick breakfast sandwich so we can get to the main station. Samantha spoke as she turned giving a playful confirming nod to her daughter.

As agreed, they stopped long enough to grab a breakfast sandwich, which each one of them had consumed by the time they turned into a very familiar community. Oh wow, Samantha barely voiced. What is it Guy asked leaning closer to hear her whispers. I so wish that I could truly explain she replied. I just felt a serious case of butterflies, feels like a band of Monarchs in route to Canada. She spoke as she giggled.

"It's really pretty here," Grae shared from the back seat. Yes sweetie, I agree. Samantha replied. Guy pulled into the driveway of their home, the one that he and Samantha had spent what seemed like countless weekends imagining, cultivating, shaping, molding and arranging years ago. Finally, today, together, they will enter into another one of there, "dreams come true," and the fact that they get to share this one with their daughter, was priceless.

"Give me one second," Guy requested as they all released their seat belt. Aaron was just heading out as Guy approached the front door. Good morning Mr. Shepherd, forgive me Sir, but it took me a little longer than I expected, I truly hoped that I would have been long gone before you and your family arrived.

It is totally okay Aaron, everything is good and your timing is just fine. So, were you able to help me out with that last minute request? Guy asked. Absolutely Sir, I believe you will find it all to your liking Aaron replied. Now, if you will excuse me Mr. Shepherd, I will be on my way. "Congratulations sir and here are yours keys. I expect that you and your family will completely enjoy your new home. If you don't mind, we will have someone to stop by and pick up that box in the foyer close to the front door." That will be fine Aaron, not a problem, and thank you. T.R.T. Reality has been absolutely a pleasure to work with throughout this whole ordeal. My family and I greatly appreciate your discretion and professionalism. Guy replied. No, it was absolutely my; our pleasure Sir, it has been a joy to be here, it is a great home, one that I am really going to miss, Aaron shared in parting. Acknowledging its passengers, he lifted his hand toward Guys vehicle as he headed to his car.

Guy returned to the vehicle, heading directly to the passenger side to open Samantha and Grae's door. "Are you guys ready?" No, excuse me, let me retract that, "are you ladies ready?" He asked with a smile as they both answered and exited the vehicle, excited about heading for the house and getting inside. "Okay, before we enter I want to try something, Guy shared. I want to carry both of you across the threshold."

Okay, who is going to be first, Grae asked? Well I guess that is where the, "try something," will come in Guy answered. You both will be first. He continued. "What are you saying?" Samantha asked. Well this should be interesting, Grae offered with a giggle.

It took a little maneuvering but, they were able to work it out and though not a great distance beyond, Guy carried his girls across the threshold. Okay someone has to capture this moment, quick someone take a picture Guy spoke in excitement. Samantha reached for her cell phone and snapped a shot. Wait one more Guy spoke, this time with kisses he spoke in laughter. With kisses, Samantha asked. "Yep, with kisses!" Guy answered. Okay Daddy, you kiss at the camera and mommy and I will kiss you on your cheek, Grae offered as an idea. So what do you say mommy, is that a deal Guy asked as he looked at Samantha. Come on mommy, say deal Grae encouraged. Well, I guess it is a deal Samantha responded giving in to the somewhat awkwardness. Okay get the camera ready, Guy spoke, and on three, first say "family" then the kisses, is everyone ready Guy asked. "1, 2, 3, Family…", and the shot was captured perfectly as the kisses were given which was a great beginning to their new home life and adventure.

"Good morning, it's the start of a productive day, are you ready to make all wrongs right?" Angie spoke in her greeting, while entering their shared office, as Sarah sat at her workstation. Humph! Now that is a loaded statement. May it be from your mouth, straight to HIS ear. Sarah replied with soft tears now dancing on her desk.

Oh no, Sarah what is it, what is going on? Angie spoke. Is there anything that I can do to help? For a few moments, the obvious emotion stole Sarah's voice so Angie moved closer with extended arms to comfort her friend. Angie, please be in prayer for my mother, my family, over the passing months one of my brothers has been in and out of the hospital twice, and we are not completely sure just what it is, that he is battling. It looks to be serious because though he has never had them before, he has been having seizures Sarah informed her officemate. Angie apologized and prayed with Sarah on the spot, but shortly after an incoming call interrupted them and Sarah used that time to step away for some much needed fresh air. Angie took the call, but her thoughts remain prayerful, for she had never seen Sarah in such a way and it concerned her. "God, only you know exactly what is set to unfold in and around about Sarah's life, please equip and prepare her for Your will as it take place. During and throughout her time of need safeguard, and keep her in her right frame of mind, allowing her to ever scenes and feel your presence. In JESUS name I pray, Amen"

For Sarah and her family, Angie had remained watchful and prayerful in the passing weeks. She was dedicated to lean to the side of keeping them extra prayed up, then not prayerfully covered enough. Until the unveiling or revealing, this is how it would be. Thankfully, Sarah sacrificially did the same for her so naturally since that day Sarah asked her to pray for her family, without question, Angie would do this for Sarah. To keep from being an office nuisance, Angie continued throughout the work day as normal as possible, but both here and at home, she often spoke Sarah's name in prayer.

It was late in the afternoon, and the end of the workweek. Sarah thought of her brother Junior a lot today. "Ump, I wonder what he has going on this evening? Maybe I can surprise him, I and could show up with dinner and a movie, and we can just hang out." Sarah quietly thought. Before she could complete that idea, her telephone rang.

Grace Confronts Her Thoughts

It was no question, that her attitude had been stinky and that, at times she thought and entertained wrong and negative thoughts. For Grace, this was not a question. This you see, Grace recognized, knew and owned completely. Though undoubtedly, she knew that she owed her husband a true and genuine apology, Grace's simple issue, was the challenge to get over Grace, long enough to genuinely extend that apology. Having to, personally deliver this apology was a whole other hurdle for her right now. To date, she had never been this challenged before to just, do right by her husband.

So why was she now? God what is this, why have I not completely graduated beyond these negative thoughts? Why am I blaming Stewart for being exactly the "who and what," our family need him to be? What more needs to be done here, or in me? God I know we have made progress in the passing months but part of me feel like I am sitting and still stewing.

Am I, ignoring something here? Be it consciously or unconsciously, am I choosing to be blind to something specific? If so, please help me. Show me how to get to the root of it because I desire to properly address and resolve this. God, is this one of those, "this kind," moments? Your word reads, "This kind only cometh by fasting and prayer." If so, help me God to map out the time and scripture of focus.

Once again, Grace found herself sitting in still silence. She thought she was right before Him, she thought she was taking the necessary steps by agreeing to talk to someone. While this, along with some other things proved helpful something was missing and she now recognized that she had managed to leave Him out of the loop on a few other things as well. At this point, it mattered not, whether or not it was intentionally. However recognizing the blessing of this self-revelation all that truly mattered was for her to have and display the proper response.

It had been a few weeks since her self-evaluation so to speak and Grace felt that she had the specifics she needed for her time of consecration so with pen and pad in hand she grabbed her bible and concordance and found a comfortable spot near the window. She made note of some fitting scripture, researched some word meanings and began to map out a prayer, while making a note of some of her needs and desires. She read through her notes once she was done, finally penning her specific and personal prayer. In the upcoming days, she and God would have many gatherings around these writings.

Stewart had a made up mind, yes. However, he later found that it was going to take more than that to come back to that place of connection that he and Grace once lived and shared.

Both he and Grace were willing and it appeared they were doing what they could, as they could to reclaim their marriage and home oasis, yet it seemed the reality of it was far off.

God what are we doing wrong, what are we missing? Wait a minute, let me began with me. So here is a do over, what am I missing, because Grace and I both know that something is missing here. Yes, Grace and I have made progress but "ump," he spoke through an extended sigh, but I don't know God I am just short of the actual words to complete that thought right now, but even with my lack of words, our end results changes not. Yes, we are kind, cordial polite and considerate of one another but Grace use to finish my sentences, I used to know her thoughts before she spoke them. Where did that go, and all of everything else that we do use to, but do not currently have go? I do not want to be angry with her, or at her but I think I am. Even though she has been right here with me, the entire time Grace has been gone, and she has been gone for too long of a time.

Be it consciously or unconsciously, I need you to help me to release and let go, of this anger and resentment. God you know better than I do, how I daily, face my wife with a smile yet it is not a genuine smile thanks to these conscious and unconscious thoughts going on in my mind. God what have I not said that I need to, what is left for us to address? We desperately need to know God because I did not sign on to this to merely, exist as a couple, or individuals that make this relationship. I will not, simply go through the motions of day-to-day life with the love of my life because of a, "disconnect".

Kevin had entered, to retrieve a few files from Stewart but since Stewart was so deep in thought with God, and self-reflection, it went unnoticed. Kevin was in and out of the office almost as soon as he had entered. "Thanks Stewart, will have these back to you in a short," Kevin spoke in his exit.

As promised, Kevin was done with the files and once again walking in Stewart's door. "Whatever it is that you are working, on must be quite interesting, I don't believe you have moved at all since I was here the first time Kevin spoke.

Ump, wait what did you just say? Stewart spoke, finally and somewhat engaging with his surroundings I mentioned how it appeared that you have not moved a bit since when I came in to grab the files. Kevin replied

So this is not your first time coming in, Stewart asked. Okay, let's push pause for a moment here, Kevin suggested. "Hey man where are you?" Tell me what is going on in that head of yours, Kevin asked.

Sadly, I do not altogether know, Stewart answered through a deep winded sigh. Before having a seat, Kevin took a few steps to close the door. Stewart, what are you talking about, just start with what you do know. Kevin encouraged. Has something happened at home? Kevin asked with concern. "Yes, and No," Stewart replied. Um I am not sure that can be, Kevin answered. I need you to keep talking.

Well it is what it has been since Grace and our children came home. Stewart spoke. I thought you and Grace were talking to someone, and you two were working it out. Yeah, that is where the gray area of "me not, altogether knowing", comes in. Stewart answered. We have conversation, we are functioning as two parents, and we collaborate about the children, the affairs of the home as well as some church stuff. I mean we are better and we are definitely making progress but sometimes it is still present Kevin. It has been like, sawing through a Sequoia with a dull butter knife. Sometimes it feels like I do not even know who my wife is, yet I love and cherish the mother of my children so much. I would walk a mile barefoot on hot coals if I had to. There, I said it to someone other than myself. I am angry over what it seems, feels like we lost. It all happened right here under both our noses. We have been present the entire time, so how could we have been so blind. How did we manage to just sit by and allow this to happen? "We have been robbed!"

Stewart, man I apologize. I had no idea; I wish I had more to offer right now, but you are my go to. What could I possible say to you that you do not already know? I mean, once you fast and pray, what more can you do? Kevin ended. You want to hear something kind of crazy Kevin, I have prayed a lot, I mean a whole lot but fasted, I have not. Stewart replied

Wait a minute say that again, Kevin requested. Yelp, you heard me right the first time Stewart replied. "Prayed, yes; fasted, no." Wow, that is unbelievable, especially after knowing and seeing that you thoughtlessly do it for others. Why would you do anything less for you and your home, why not take the same measures for the need of your family? Kevin offered. I guess sometimes, the obvious, is not so obvious to the one that it should be obvious to. It was not a thought to me, for me to fast on this, but I will start preparing myself this evening. Thanks my friend, and you thought you would need to offer something more. Well, you said exactly what needed to be said Kevin. It was *exactly*

what was needed", Stewart repeated softly in a moment of self-reflection.

Okay so tell me, how are things with you? Stewart asked aiming to redirect the conversation.

Chapter Four

Thank God For My Girls

Grace found that having what she said she wanted, had both its payoffs and its drawbacks, but even with the drawbacks, she chose to welcome and embrace each moment of being a mother and having her little ones home where they belonged. Whew, thank you God for this, and other answered prayers, You are so awesome to me! With the breath of this verbal praise, still warm upon her lips, Grace soon after heard the outcry of one of her little ones. "Mommy's coming," she called out, and down the hall she went. During her short trip down the hall, the telephone rang but Grace opted to see about her little one first. "Whoever is calling will have to wait a few minutes," she softly voiced.

By now Samantha had moved mostly all that she needed into the house, the place she and Guy built, first on paper, then in reality so many years ago. Alongside of Guy, she and Grae now called this place home.

Wow, it was true, this was all real, they were a family and Samantha was getting use to the idea of being a wife, a mother, and a new home owner, she was once again remembering how to be , and learning in some ways, how to be a sister and friend!

"Man, not that I am complaining God, but this is a lot." Whew, she released in a sigh. Before she could escape in this thought the home telephone, begin to ring.

Hello, Samantha answered. Samantha this is Grace. Wow Grace I had almost forgotten how nurturing and calming your voice is on the telephone. Samantha greeted. Ha, ha ha, you are too sweet Samantha, thank you although here lately you may be the only one that would speak these words. Grace shared with a soft chuckle. "But you know what, that is a long story, one to be explored on another day. Anyway, Samantha we have missed you so much. It is so great to be able to pick up the telephone and call you again. Oh my goodness, and little Miss Grae, she is such a sweetheart, I have about five years of spoiling to catch up on! What are you doing right now, Kathy doesn't know it yet but she and I want to come over as soon as you are available! Samantha welcomed Grace's excitement, love, care, and interest with laughter, wait what do you mean, "Kathy doesn't know yet?" Samantha asked. Only that since she's been so distracted from her friend by her new business endeavor that she could not be reached in my attempts to reach her today before my calling you. What new business Samantha asked? You know what, hold that thought, Grace replied. Can you hold on the line a few moments, she requested of Samantha. Sure, Samantha answered.

Since Grace felt it was worth it she called to get Kathy on the phone while she had Samantha on the line.

"Hello, Kathy Speaking." Really Kathy, why so formal, Grace spoke in response to Kathy's greeting. Grace Adam if you do not act right I am going to drop your call Kathy replied in laughter. What is up with you today, Kathy continued. So glad you asked Grace answered. Don't you want to accompany me to Guy's and Samantha's and officially welcome her back? Yeah great, what day next week are we going to do this, Kathy asked. Well what better time than the present, I mean like now the current present, like literally, right now, Grace suggested. Wait, are you saying within the next couple of hours, or right now, this very moment, right now Kathy asked. I'm leaning toward the later, Grace answered. Where are you, I can pick you up or you can meet me there, you do know how to get to the new house right? The new house, what new house Kathy asked. You cannot be   serious   right   now   Kathy, where have you been, Grace asked. That is right, how could I forget. Lately, it seems that, "K-E-P," gets any time Kevin and Kaye leaves behind. Grace smugly replied. What, Kathy enquired?

Oops, wait a minute, girl I have Samantha on hold. Let me check on her, give me a minute Grace requested of Kathy. Pshh please, do not play yourself. Grace you know Sam hung up the minute you clicked over, you get long winded Grace. Kathy managed to offer before Grace could click over to the other line.

"Samantha, are you still there, hello. Hello? Just as Kathy Had predicted Samantha had left the telephone conversation. Okay Kathy, I am back. Hello, Hello, Kathy, Kathy, oh no she didn't Grace spoke."

Ha, ha, ha, you are right, I didn't Kathy finally revealed with laughter. I apologize to you Grace, but I could not refuse the chance to laugh a little at your expense. So, what's up chick, you ready to ride out? Kathy continued jokingly. I am headed to your house as we speak Kathy ended. Okay, well by for now girl, I need to do a few things before leaving. Safe travels, and see you in a short. Grace spoke before placing her phone to rest.

With excitement about being able to sit down and catch up with Samantha at the forefront of her mind, swiftly Grace moved through her home, doing what needed to be done. Shortly after, just as advised, Kathy arrived and they were now loaded up, and in route to see Samantha Shepherd.

Remembering a few of Samantha's favorite things, all that Grace and Kathy did not have on hand, would be taken care of with a short telephone call and a brief stop.

Renewed

Knowing that Grace would call her back, Samantha moved around the house adding some final touches through the house. She found herself, humming at times even singing, a relaxing warm melody. "We're in this love together…"

Now making her way to the bedroom she realized a great deal of time had gone by and still no call back from Grace. "Oh, so she's not calling me back?" Samantha thought aloud, walking toward the telephone. As she reached for the telephone, she noticed a vehicle slowing in front of their home and eventually pulling into the driveway. She stopped what she was doing, and stood for a bit in front of the window, "maybe they are just turning around," she thought. When the vehicle continued the path of her driveway and closer to the house, Samantha was able to make out Grace Adam. Well, well, well, so they are gonna just show up unannounced hum. Ha, ha, oh I am soo gonna get them. Let me see, Samantha softly spoke as she looked around her immediate area.

Giving it a quick thought Samantha grabbed the bottle from the gift basket they received from T.R.T. realty, pouring some of the contents upon herself as well as the floor. She quickly, unlocked the door, moved back near the small puddle on the floor, lying down next to it with an empty glass. There on the floor she remained, being as still as she possible could as she awaited their arrival at the door. Finally, Samantha could hear their footsteps and playful chatter. Making herself as serious and lifeless looking as she could, she braced herself for their eventual entry.

Grace rang the doorbell, after no answer she rang again. Grace maybe you should knock to, Kathy suggested. "Still no answer, what are you doing Sam?" Grace softly spoke as she continues to ring the doorbell and knock. "Where is she, Grace she is expecting us right?" Kathy asked, turning to Grace for confirmation. Um, well… wait a minute Grace, Kathy interrupted stealing Grace's chance to speak. Grace, did Samantha clearly state, now is a good time for our visit, or did Grace Adam come up with that on her own? She concluded.

Well, not really. Grace answered. What, "Not really," Kathy asked. Well I don't think I ever, really, directly said that we were trying to come over today, well rather, right now. Grace finally, straightly answered. "Seriously Grace?" Kathy thought aloud.

Wait; just wait a minute Kathy, before you get all fussy I will get her on the phone. Grace replied. Grace, do we even know that Samantha is here? Kathy managed to ask through a breathy sigh. Hold, hold on I am calling her now, Grace replied while waiting for the call to go through. Well do you have an emergency key? Kathy asked as she passively and thoughtlessly, landed a single knock while trying to open the door. To her surprise, the door was unlocked so she slowly pushed the door open. "Hello, Samantha." She called out getting no response. Before completely opening the door, Kathy checked with Grace to see if she was able to get Samantha on the phone. "No. No answer." Grace informed, but maybe she knew we would get here before her return so she left the door unlocked. Grace suggested. But Grace, you just said Samantha wasn't really expecting us. Kathy reminded. I know, but we are here, and the doors is open, let us just go inside and wait. Grace suggested as she opened the door wide enough for her to step inside.

With less than two steps inside, Grace yelled out. Oh my god, Kathy spoke as she and Grace moved closer to Samantha noticing her lying motionless on the floor. Almost simultaneously, Grace and Kathy took turns calling out Samantha's name, encouraging her to wake up, and get up or at least speak, but they got nothing. Samantha gave no response.

Oh no Kathy, what do we do? Grace spoke with great concern. Really Grace; really, you are asking me that question? Grace you are the one that is buddy-buddy with God. Kathy spoke with conviction. "Seriously Kathy? Seriously," Grace asked.

Yeah, seriously Grace, I did not stutter! "Seriously you two, I could be dying her!" Samantha finally spoke. "What?", both Kathy and Grace spoke almost rhythMiccilly.

"Gotcha!" Samantha resumed in laughter. As she reached out to hug Grace and Kathy, "come here you too, show me some love!" Samantha spoke with more laughter. Move girl this little prank is not funny Grace spoke as she positioned herself to get up from the floor.

No! Move Samantha, I do not want to laugh, your silly self. You have my heart racing and my nerves are a wreck! Do not even touch me, right now. I will hug you later. Maybe, Grace spoke. You ought to be living right Grace, then your nerves would not be tore up right about now!

On that note, Kathy could no longer contain her laughter, and she released it from the bottom of her stomach. Be quite Kathy what are you laughing at. Grace poutingly spoke. Samantha you were wrong for this one though Kathy continued, I cannot began to explain the range of emotions I experienced just now. Whew, you wrong for that, Grace spoke. I just might keep the goodies we brought for you!

You mean you two came bearing gifts. Samantha asked. Well what other way could we come? Grace asked in a softer tone attempting to move pass Samantha's silly prank. "Oh, so Grace you are talking to me now, we friends once again?" Samantha naggingly, yet playfully asked. Until the very end Grace spoke. Awe Grace, Samantha interjected. "Whether I like you or not," Grace finished. Ha ha ha, they all laughed as they shared a group hug. Once the three connected in a friendly embrace, the reality of the moment hit home and touched them individually one by one. In a short amount of time, the laughter turned into sobbing and the sobbing faded into streams of tears all around.

Grace and Kathy spent the day showering Samantha with love, prayers, more tears and laughter. They spent time catching her up on their lives, and shared in on some of her favorite things. Thanks to it being, "Daddy and me day," the children were accounted for, and would be well taken care of which meant, these women had nowhere to be, no time soon.

Daddy and Me

The guys decided they would all meet at the same place, on their, daddy and me outing, giving them a little time to, plug in and offer Stewart some much-needed support with the twins while the rest of the children had fun.

"So Grace, what are you going to cook, because we are going to need something to eat," Kathy asked. "Um nothing, if it has to do with me," Grace answered. I am a guess Kathy look around, this ain't my house. And yes, I just said, "ain't." Grace spoke with playful laughter. Grace you cannot be serious, we are going to need something to eat soon. You playing, Kathy replied. Kathy, I am a guest, the guest is not supposed to come in off the street, right into someone's kitchen. Besides, this is my first visit. Um, baby steps Kathy, baby steps! Well Samantha what are you gonna cook because it is almost time for us to eat. Kathy informed.

You know what I honestly like the idea of your question being directed to Grace, but in the same breath, I am not sure if I should be offended, at least a little for you not asking me first. I mean as Grace pointed out; she is the guest here, Samantha spoke with a chuckle. Samantha just stop! I mean how fair is it, for two people to show up unexpectedly, expecting a host and cook too. I mean, with this visit being Graces idea I think it is the least she can do, and should do. Kathy explained. "Um hello, did I leave the room or something?" Kathy I do not know what to do with you sometimes Grace spoke with a genuine smile.

All jokes aside though, we did tell you that we came bearing gifts so I did come prepared to whip together a quick dish. So if you do not already have meal plans just point me in the right direction Grace spoke. Awe Grace you still are one of the best. I would love for you to prepare a quick dish for us. Before we head to the kitchen, first we must take a tour of the house. Samantha replied. Finally, Kathy spoke out; I thought I was going to have to ask for the tour. Whew, it is about time! Kathy ended. Hush Kathy! Samantha spoke with laughter, as she softly tugged on both of their arms, come on.

Other than the fact that they would all meet, the men, had not spent a lot of time planning this day for them and the children, now finished with breakfast, Guy and Grae were the first to arrive at the decided meeting point. After about ten minutes, Grae finally ask "Daddy aren't we going inside, we have been sitting here for a while now." Grae sweetly spoke. "I do apologize, what was that milady?" Guy playfully asked catching a view of Grae's face from the rear view mirror. "Daddee, Grae softly sang. Yelp, that's what you call me Guy teasingly spoke "I like it when you call me daddee," Guy playfully continued with animation. Seem, just as I figured you did here me, Grae spoke. Yeah, I did, but at least I began with an apology, see now it is you not listening. "Really Daddy?" Grae spoke playfully looking back at him by way of the rearview mirror with squinted eyes.

Okay kiddo, all joking aside. Since we were the first to arrive, I figured there was no need to rush inside, let me make a few calls sweetie. There may have been some last minute change. Guy made his calls and upon the completion of them, he shared the last minute update that he received from Kevin. Well, we have a slight change in plans Grace. Well now what, Grae asked. According to Kevin, instead of here, we are going to meet at Kolin's house. Who is Kolin, Grae asked. That's Kevin's brother. I am not exactly sure what has been decided after that, but we should arrive in a short. Back on the road we go. Guy shared as he informed Grae of their next move.

Guy and Stewart both received the word and were in route to Kolin's house. Soon after both arrived in what seemed like a matter of minutes apart.

More Girl Time

Grace had forgotten how well the trusted women in her life knew her, though only a short time in her presence, Samantha had already sensed a heaviness about Grace, which at some point in the evening she would find the right time to point it out.

As they gathered in the kitchen, Grace assigned both Kathy and Samantha a task to help move the preparation along while she focused on the cooking. They filled their time of work with a lot of talking and laughter. Some of which, was at the expense of their husbands.

Daddy and Me

Pulling up to Kolin's home, Grae shared her appreciation of it's outer beauty. Daddy, who did you say lives here. She asked. Kevin's brother Kolin. Guy answered.

Wow, I really like this Grae shared. What are we going to do her? Well Grae I guess we will soon find out. Why don't we go inside, Guy encouraged. Once they reached the door, Guy had Grae ring the doorbell.

My Girls and Me

Okay, ladies the wait is over. Let's eat! Grace proclaimed. Happy to oblige, they passed the prepared dishes assembled on the table and fixed their plate. Giving Samantha the honor of blessing the meal, mealtime was in full swing.

What a meal. It seemed that Kathy and Samantha could not praise Grace enough. Everything she prepared was beyond good. When Samantha and Kathy attempted to help themselves to a third helping, Grace stopped them. "Wait minute ladies, just so you know, you are more than welcome to help yourselves to more but before you load your plates be advised, we do have dessert prepared to."

"Dessert, Samantha asked. I didn't expect dessert to." "Well I did, Kathy chimed in but I would not have asked, had it not been mentioned. Thank you so much Grace, see that's one of the reasons you are a keeper." Kathy shared jokingly. "So what are we having," she concluded.

You will see soon enough, now come on ladies, we all know that a Grace Adam meal is incomplete if it does not include dessert. Grace responded. Here, help me clear these dinner dishes, and make room for dessert. They traded their plates, Samantha slipped back into the kitchen, discreetly beginning a little pre-cleaning, while Grace and Kathy assembled the table for dessert. Okay, let's do this. Samantha where did you go, get in here dessert is served. Enjoy dear hearts!

The evening continued as they sat at the table savoring there, sweet treat. Once again, Kathy and Samantha could not thank Grace enough for the joy they experienced, thanks to their Grace Adam dessert.

So Grace, tell me, what is it that I missed, what exactly is going on in your world?

Samantha asked. Hey, I think I want something hot to drink, you do have coffee or tea right, Kathy asked suggestively. Yes. We actually have both; everything you will need should be located in the cabinet above the water kettle. Samantha confirmed. Now Grace back to you. So, tell me about you. Samantha continued as she refreshed her previous question.

Funny Samantha, you say that like there is something to tell Grace replied. Well sounds like your response is a confirmation there is something to tell, but I have been cut off from my family and friends for some time, so I apologize if I am out of line, or seem to be prying, Samantha shared.

Well Kathy, what about you, catch me up girl. Samantha spoke softly giving her a nudge. Wow, we get to talk about me, cool! Kathy spoke with excitement. Well, to start, not too long ago Kevin had a scary incident when his tire blew out as he was driving along. We got a call from Kaye's school, after seeing that Kaye was having a rough time dealing with the unexpected death of one of the schools most loved volunteers. Her teacher asked if we would come and check on Kaye. The very same day, while in route back to the office...wait a minute, how did we manage to be on Kathy right now when my question was on the table? Grace softly, yet directly asked.

Oh, well that would be my fault Grace, forgive me but I got the impression that you had nothing you wanted to share. Kathy, do you mind if we push pause on your time of sharing for a few, I did began by asking Grace a question, and we do want to do things in decency and in order. Samantha spoke. The floor is yours Grace, please speak on, Kathy offered.

Okay, see now you two are joking me. Grace spoke with a chuckle, but guess what, I am going to, "take the floor, and speak on," as Kathy put it. "Now, let me see; I guess we can begin a few weeks before our babies were born…" Kathy and Samantha made eye contact, sneaking in a "congratulatory wink" of the eye in their smooth, indirect way to get Grace to willingly, open up and freely speak. Grace, indeed took the floor, and favorably, she had it for some time, even with all that she shared, revealed confessed and owned, in her sharing about herself, in Kathy and Samantha's opinion her strength and faith, yet remained in tack. It may have sound and felt like weakness to Grace, but to her true friends, it sound like tremendous strength. They had no words to properly, relay the level of honor, love, and respect they had and possessed for her. They had loved her in the past, and they would continue to love her, here now and beyond.

That evening, so much was shared, not that it was intentional, but it had been quite some time since Grace had been as open, unguarded and transparent. It was never her intention to close out her friends, and especially not her husband, but somehow, that is exactly what she had managed to do. In addition to, what great compassion, love, support and help, she had missed out on. It was like second nature to give this, to be this, to those Grace loved, but somewhere down the line her, "I don't want to be a bother, or I will just figure it or work it out," attitude and mindset, turned into Grace against the world. This type of atmosphere was not what she had planned or what she wanted encamped around her. Up until Samantha's disappearance, Samantha and Kathy had always been there for her, and it was wonderful to have Samantha back home, where she belonged, with them. Though a few things had changed, the fact that she still knew those special trigger words and actions that encouraged Grace to sing like a canary was as sharp, if not sharper as ever! "Welcome back Samantha, welcome back." Grace silent thought.

"Whew, Lord I thank you," Okay then Kathy, the floor is all yours! Grace proclaimed, feeling almost 20 pounds lighter. With great laughter from all, Kathy decided to take a rain check. "Grace, whatever," after what we just experienced, that's almost like calling a fellow congregant up to preach, a sweeping move of the holy spirit." I do have a suggestion though, how about a little stroll through Samantha's neighborhood? Kathy shared. Wait a minute, do you have an adult size stroller, because you two may have to carry me! Grace jokingly inserted. "Really Grace, really?" Samantha and Kathy both asked, "Get on up," Kathy playfully continued as Samantha concluded with a whistle. Awe, you remembered, Kathy sighed as she reached in, playfully nudging Samantha as they shared the memory of an old school song. Okay girls let's get our walk on. Grace spoke, more so, encouraging herself.

Daddy and Me

Conveniently equipped, with a pool and lots of space for everyone, meeting at Kolin's turned out to be a great last minute change. The only question now, what was everyone going to eat. Daddy I am getting hungry, are we going to eat soon? Good question Grae, one that I honestly do not have the answer to, let me check with the rest of the fellows to hear what the plan is. Guy offered as he stepped away.

Okay fellas I don't know if Grae is the only one asking, but I am asking for the both of us if so; what are we gonna do about eating. Guy asked Kevin. Do not worry Guy we got everyone covered. Kolin will be bringing some things in when he return. Actually, it should not be too much longer before he arrives. He has already called ahead, asking dad to ready the grills. Okay, is there something you want me to do? Guy asked. Not at the moment, but should that change we will find you. Kevin replied. Fair enough, Guy responded as he returned to Grae with the update.

My Girls and Me

"I don't think I've entertain a stroll like this since Stewart and I brought the twins home, um." Grace concluded a long with a sigh.

Grace, respectfully I am going to," get in your business" by asking you this but, why is it that the mentioning of your husband's name just now seemed to weaken your smile? Samantha asked. "Wow, you went right there didn't you," Kathy softly yet directly spoke. Yes I did, because "right there" as you put it Miss Kathy is exactly where Grace needs to go, whether she choose to answer my question, or not. It does not erase the fact that eventually Grace will need to honestly, answer the question.

By now, the graceful stride of their steps had come to a halt, a complete stop.

Daddy and Me

Though enduring some minor adjustments, daddy and me day was full of fun, laughter, games, good food and great company. After adjusting, their day had unfolded rather quickly once they arrived at Kolin's. By now, the day was preparing for the night but the children were still hard at play and the adults, though nearby, were just as much at play. While the others were laughing, eating, chatting, and simply enjoying the evening, Guy seized the chance to personally, thank Kolin. The group at "T.W.K." was excited about this new business paring, and looking forward to great things from the group at K-3 Horizon. Though it would have been easy for Guy to expand the conversation into talks of the actually project, he drew the line in his mind to keep it from becoming talks about work. Guy ended almost as quickly as he began, with his statement of thank you.

It was good to see that this proved to be a great last minute idea. It was a great meeting place for all. Momma Koole had been hanging out with the smaller children, almost, from the time of her and poppa Kooles arrival.

To offer momma Koole a little break, periodically through the course of the day the adults and older children came over to their little fort allowing her the time she needed to step away. Though both the, children and the adults were well aware that it was time to shut down the fun and games, and transition to clean up, neither wanted to say so. Mother Koole, on the other hand, was the attentive one. Being aware of the soon approaching night, and armed with the motivation of taking her sweetie-pie home, she did not mind actively bringing it to everyone's attention. The smaller children had been a delight to care for, and everyone else had been thoughtful throughout the day, but momma Koole was ready to head home and relax with poppa Koole.

To get the ball fully in motion, she got up and began the initiative knowing that Kolin would kick in and take over once he saw his mom working on cleaning up. Momma Koole began the effort, but shortly after both she and her husband were encouraged to just take it easy, and head home for some rest. It happened exactly as she thought it would, and soon after their good night kisses and hugs, she and poppa Koole were soon on their way. "Good night, we love you all dearly!"

Strolling With My Girls

Okay, we can shelf the question, but we need you to pinpoint the "it," what is it Grace? Has he abandoned you, leaving you to mother and look after the children alone? What is it? Samantha asked. "Look Grace none of us are perfect, that's normally the assumed perception of the one outside looking in. I find it hard to believe that the Stewart I remember is walking around your home with that type of attitude. I mean, I am not in your home, you are, but that is still hard for me to believe. However, again as stated before, I don t know, "what you know, like you know it". Samantha replied. Well let me map it out for you, when it comes down to our children he has all the answers, he understands every sound they make. Since the children has come home he has turned into Mr. Perfect, Super-Dad, it is just sickening almost, Grace spoke lapping her eyes.

So Grace are you saying that because it appears to you that your husband has a better handle on parenthood, with a shorter adjustment and adaptation, in some ways at the moment better than you, that he feels or thinks that he is "Mr. Perfect" at it? Samantha concluded with a chuckle, but having realized it was an outward expression, quickly apologized. Excuse me Grace; yes, I have a chuckle in my response but not at your situation or expense. "Well you are doing a good job of fooling me," Grace interrupted. No, seriously, Samantha confirmed resuming her response.

Grace, I have never known you to do anything halfway. You have always been specific, intentional, reliable, dependable, direct, dedicated, loyal, committed and even adjustable and flexible as needed. Now, the person that I just described is still 100% the Grace Adam that I know, but do you believe that still. Would you say that here lately, or right now, that you are or that you have been, thinking and functioning as, 100%-Grace Adam?

I personally find this hard to believe because the 100-Grace Adam, would never consciously throw shade at her husband, especially when, without hesitation, he steps up and pitch in to be exactly what and who you and your family need him to be. Come on Grace, when you and your babies came home, what other response would you have wanted form your husband? Don't be angry at him for being and doing, who and what you have spent all the time up until such a time as this, or that, encouraging, and coaching him to be.

So Grace, tell me what is so wrong with that? Is he not doing, being the him, God, in answering your prior prayer, cultivated and molded him to be, the one man, friend and husband that you've, in and with wisdom, have loved him to be?

Um girl, I needed to have been recording this, repeat all of that, Kathy jokingly yet sincerely blurted out while snapping her fingers and reaching for her cell phone. Almost instantly, they were overtaken by a timely, and much needed moment of laughter, after such a heavy moment.

Stop acting silly Kathy, Samantha replied playfully as she softly nudged Kathy. Samantha I am for real! You had me over here reflecting and I am not even the one being, well ya know. She ended.

"Go on and finish it, what Kathy, being what?' Grace asked. I opt to leave that alone, besides Samantha has given us both a lot to marinate in, Kathy replied. Whew. I guess you do have a point Grace spoke, but at some point I want to hear the rest of your thought, she concluded. Samantha, Samantha, Samantha, I know you cannot see it and you may not be able to tell it, but I am reduced to nubs right about now. Grace shared. "Nubs?" Samantha asked. Yeah, because you stepped on my feet so bad, causing my toes to curled up to barely being nubs. Shoot, in fact,

I am surprised that I am still able to stand! Thank God for Kathy's outburst, because at that moment, the laughter is exactly what I needed.

Samantha you shared, exactly what needed to be shared. Here I am, believing this visit was all about welcoming you back with us, and it turned into this. You are right, so long ago; Stewart, my husband was cultivated, and prepared for such a time as this. I know it is not obvious, nor is it properly displayed, but at the core of my being, I am proud of my husband, and I value, greatly all that he has proved and shown to be. I am upset and disappointed with me. I am disappointed with all of my shortcomings, and failures in this life chapter, and my strained transitional adjustments to these additional, life roles.

Not only is this the first time I've had to take a back seat to Stewart in our home, but it's the first time that I've had to watch him from the sideline do everything better. I feel like I do not fit in our home. Therefore, instead of my husband's perfection, I guess it is my vase range of imperfection that, I see when I look at him. Right now, I don't know how to live, and function in this place, in the same space with him. Grace softly concluded. Well thank God for that Kathy encouraged, because you finally know what it is and recognize that this is a temporary place. You cannot and will not, park here Grace Adam. Besides, with "Warden Samantha" around, I suspect that would be close to impossible!

Unable to suppress it any longer, Grace was overtaken with emotion, and finally sweetly ushered into a place of complete release. This was something greatly needed and long overdue. Samantha and Kathy moved closer, embracing Grace in a warm welcomed hug. "Awe, come here Grace, but turn your head that way and snot on Samantha, after all she is the one that made you cry. Kathy spoke softly. Come on Grace, Samantha encouraged, while respecting the moment, but seizing the opportunity to shoot some sharp eyes at Kathy, something, with Kathy being Kathy, she received with a smile.

Daddy and Me

Okay people, operation clean up is underway! Kolin informingly announced, let the clean up begin, he concluded. With everyone pitching in, everything was soon in order and back in its rightful place. Everyone headed inside for one last bathroom break before loading up in their vehicles, heading for their individual destinations.

Okay Grae, we need to head for home, be sure to say thank you to Kevin's brother Kolin for allowing us to hang out at his house today. Guy reminded. Absolutely, thank you Mr. Kolin I had a lot of fun here. Grae shared. Thank you, that is good to hear Grae you are welcome, and you and your family are welcome here anytime. We will have to see when we can all do this again won't we, Kolin concluded. Sure, Grae agreed as she said goodnight to everyone on her way out. I agree with Grae, I believe we all had a great time Thanks so much Kolin, Guy sealed with a hand shake. I really could do this again, he concluded. Guy gave his good night greeting to all, and headed for his vehicle.

Now that Kevin was certain that everything was good with his brother, nephew and the home, they headed out two. Stewart and the twins had tagged alone with Kevin and Kaye, making them the last guest to leave. Kolin saw them out, bidding them a good night with safe travels. "Hey I want to hear from you once you make it home," Kolin called out to Kevin as he pulled off. "Okay," Kevin replied. I love you man, thanks for everything. Kevin concluded as he continued on his way.

Along the commute to Stewart's home, Kevin's phone rang. "Hello," he answered. "Well hello yourself," Kathy replied. "Listen, why did you not answer the home phone, better yet, why haven't you called to check in on me?" She jokingly concluded. "Well, one I am not home, and two we totally lost track of time. The children were having so much fun that we felt bad rounding everyone up to head home he replied with a chuckle. Wait a minute, where are you at this hour, and why did you not call and check in on your husband and daughter? Kevin asked Kathy playfully. I will tell you all about my day later, where exactly are you two? Kathy replied. We are on our way to drop Stewart and the twins off, and then Kaye and I will head for home Kevin answered. Hey, since I am riding with Grace, heading to her house, I can just hop in with you and Kay, once I get there, do you mind waiting for me if you get there before me? Kathy asked. "Umm, actually I do, as a matter of fact we both feel that way with the day being as long and busy as it was. Kevin answered." "What?" Wait a minute what did you just say Mr. Koole! Kathy passionately asked. Yelp, you heard me correctly, Kevin replied, holding in the laughter. "But baby I promise you, I was only joking, he quickly spoke to fill the air as it begin to thicken." For you, I would spring out of bed and dash to the car at 3 in the morning, to be exactly where you want me." We will see you after a while Kevin concluded with a chuckle. Yeah, I hear you Mr. Koole I love you two, Kathy spoke. We love you back Kevin replied before ending the call.

Pulling into the Adams driveway, Kevin asked Stewart what he wanted him to do. Let me just take one of them at a time if you do not mind waiting, Steward answered. Of course we do not mind, take your time, as a matter of fact you may as well go ahead and get her situated for bed. Besides, Kaye and I are going to hold tight for Grace and Kathy to arrive. When Kathy heard that we would be dropping you off, she decided she would just ride home with Kaye and I. Guess we will figure out her car later. So again, there is no rush man, I mean that. Yeah you have a point, that's right, thank you. I almost forgot that Grace was still out. Maybe I will be able to get them both taken care of before Grace gets in. That way she will not have to be bothered when she arrives.

In record time, Stewart had managed to maneuver the late evening, bedtime ritual and tasks for his daughter, but still he was not quite fast enough. As he headed back to Kevin's vehicle for his son, Grace was already stepping inside with him bidding the Koole family safe travels home.

Hey Stewart, I am guessing today was a good outing for everyone since we all are pretty much just making it home. If you are not too tired, I would like to hear about your day once I get our son situated. Grace offered. For a brief moment, Stewart did not know if he should be relieved, or disturbed that Grace may be feeling that this talk was something she had to make herself do. Was he supposed to encourage this talk? He was not sure if he was disappointed or grateful that she had accepted ownership of this task, but even still, he managed to smile politely as he gave her room to pass by. "Okay, I will see you in the room," he spoke as he continued, slowly bypassing the baby's room.

Stewart grabbed a few things and headed for the shower, he utilized these moments wisely, as he truthfully surveyed his thoughts. He remembered, the talk and prayer some time ago as he requested both sets of hands, "all aboard and actively working," now that it appeared to be taking place he now found himself praying that God would help him to, genuinely possess and display the right attitude and spirit as he welcomed his wife's input and help. Regardless of how awkward it felt, it was still what he needed and wanted.

Grace had become more and more active with the children since that day of reflection while sitting alone in the kitchen, but it still felt like she had to have Stewart's permission to do anything for or with her babies.

Tonight was different and it genuinely felt like a team working together. Not only did Grace want more enter changes like this, but she was looking forward to them and committed to surrendering herself that it would happen. Finally, she was actually seeing the necessary change she believed would take place, and so desperately needed to see, "thank you God for what you have and will continue to do in our home, marriage, life, mind, and heart." Having her son cared for and tucked in for the night, Grace headed to her bedroom.

Wow God, thank you for never giving up on me, and not letting me park in that dark place. She expressed in quiet gratitude. As still tears collect in her eyes, she now watched her husband entering their bedroom from the bathroom.

Hey Grace, is everything okay? Stewart asked noticing his teary-eyed wife. Yes, she softly spoke. Okay, I will not be pushy but as always, I am here, whatever the need may be. Grace gave a nod of her head in her best effort to respond, as she stood still, in her quite moment of gratitude.

It was a long day for us all hum? Stewart asked in attempt to redirect the mood. Yeah, but it was a good, long day, one that you welcome and embrace, because of the way it was spent and because of the people you got to spend it with. Grace replied. Exactly, your day sounds a lot like our day. I am all done, if you need the bathroom Stewart spoke as he passed Grace, cordially placing his hand on her shoulder. Okay, I need to grab a few things first. Thank you love, Grace replied with a sweet, playful wink.

Grace grabbed her things found her way to the bathroom and later joined her husband. Stewart, will you lead us in prayer before we call it a night, Grace sweetly yet firmly suggested. After prayer, they shared a good night kiss, with both of them finding that comfortable resting place.

Stewart? Grace called out softly. Are you sleep, she asked while extending a soft poking with her finger into his shoulder. Not quit, he answered. You sound tired Grace replied. Why put off for tomorrow what we can do now? Talk to me, what is on your mind Stewart replied as he set up in bed doing his best to be alert and render his full attention to his wife.

Stewart, can we talk, Grace longingly asked. "Why, you want to know my name," Stewart playfully asked. "You better tell me your name baby…," Grace managed to sing in response with a soft warm smile. See, that is just one of the reasons why I love you boy, she continued in her playful tone sealing it with a wink. Ha, ha, ha, thank you, I know that you love me Grace; I love you to. Now tell me, what exactly are we going to talk about tonight? Well let me start with a very sincere, and much needed apology. Grace spoke preparing herself to openly and honestly discuss her thoughts, and share the things of her heart.

It was a long, full night, but by the end of the conversation; both Grace and Stewart had taken time to openly share and discuss all they knew that needed to be shared.

By the time Kathy and Kevin reached home that night, Kaye was sound asleep. Kathy felt bad about awakening her but it had to be done because in no way was she about to let Kaye crawl into bed without a shower. "Okay, Kevin you get Kaye up and to the shower, while I will go get her night clothes and pull her covers back, Kathy offered as a quick game plan while opening her door and exiting the vehicle just as fast. " Oh! oh no you didn't; now why do I have to be the bad guy? Let me get her clothes and pull back the covers" Kevin pleaded to the now closed door. Left to be the bad guy, Kevin did what he had to do. "Kaye we are home sweetie, I tell you what, Daddy will carry you inside but once we get there I need you to take your shower before bed okay?" Though slow and very sluggish in her response, Kaye gave a compliant okay. Kaye, okay sweetie, here you go. Your mom has placed your clothes her on the counter, I am going to my room. If you need anything, let us know. Okay daddy, thank you. Kaye answered. You are welcome, I love you Kaye. I love you too daddy. Good night, they both bid one another.

You know you owe me right! Kevin announced loudly as he entered their bedroom. What was that, Kathy asked as she turned off the water. Yeah, you know that you heard me. Kevin confirmed. Okay, okay, just send me the bill Kevin. Kathy replied with laughter, now go get cleaned up I will check in on Kay and meet you back here.

Kathy Is Sweetly Encouraged

Momma, it is a good thing that you got here just in time, I was about to say my prayers. Kaye invitingly shared. Okay great, mommy is just in time; you start us off. After prayer Kaye gave her mommy a good night kiss and soon after her head meet the pillow, "sleep therapy" stepped in.

Though not sleep yet, Kevin was already in bed when Kathy returned. "Really, it is like that, so you are going to go to sleep on me." Kathy spoke as she entered the room. Getting no answer, she took that as her answer. Before she could comfortably position herself in bed, her husband began to snore. "Oh wow, are you serious?" Kathy softly voiced. Yelp, I am serious her husband softly replied with laughter. Gotcha! Kevin continued with more laughter. "Good night, give me a kiss!" "Ain't, now laugh at that," Kathy replied jokingly as she leaned in to meet her husband for a good night kiss."

Chapter Five

Grateful

Blessed to have friends like Grace and Kathy, thinking about them and their acts of kindness and love warmed Samantha's heart. She was so glad they made time for her and the surprise visit was better than anything that she could have planned. That is until their visit she had forgotten how much they brought into and added to her day-to-day life when they were all together. Thank you Samantha spoke aloud, looking upward. It is good to be home, it is so good to be home. She spoke as she surveyed her surroundings. She heard Guy and Grae entering, as she sat quietly enjoying the sweetness of this thought. "Samantha, were home," Guy softly spoke as he carried Grae inside. Hey, you two, Samantha spoke as she surfaced in the hallway. "Where do you want me to put her?" Guy asked. Baby we are gonna have to wake her for her bath Samantha informed. Samantha, can she not just do that in the morning? Guy asked. She is tired, Guy added. No baby, hand her over, because this little missy is off to the shower. "Come on Grae, wake up sweetie, I know it's late but it's bath time," Samantha advised as she and Grae disappeared into the bathroom.

When Samantha Made it to their room, Guy had already freshened up and comfortably resting in bed. Are you asleep; Samantha asked her husband as she crawled into bed? Not totally, he answered. "But wait a minute, before you get too comfortable, um did you shower yet?" He asked as he playfully used a stiff arm to block her access to bed. What, Samantha asked. "Yelp, I just asked you if you had your night time bath yet, besides if it was a, fitting enough request of little exhausted Grae, how much so for her mother in making sure that she shower before bed?" Guy shared. Oh, so that's how we do, Samantha asked. "That's how we do," Guy answered. "I can't just shower in the morning?" Samantha suggested. No, you need to take care of that tonight. Guy replied with a chuckle. "Come on, would you like an escort?" He continued. No, I do not need an escort Samantha replied. For the record, I took care of that before you two late arrivals, made it home this evening. Really, Guy asked. Are you sure? "Yes baby!" Samantha answered with a smirk.

Oh, well okay then, bed access granted. I love you, good night. Guy shared kissing his wife goodnight. I wanted to tell you all about our daddy and me day but I am too tired for a meaningful conversation. Guy concluded before finding a more comfortable spot. Trust, I completely understand. I would love to tell you about my unexpected visit from Grace and Kathy, we had such a great evening but like you, right now the only thing I am good for is sleep. Let's share our day in the morning, deal? Deal, Guy managed to reply. Good night, I love you too. Samantha spoke before closing her eyes in sleep.

The next morning, Guy's eyes, were opened first. After staring at the ceiling for a few moments, Guy propped up on his side and lovingly looked over upon his wife. Being reminded of HIS grace and mercy, Guy spent these precious moments with God until Samantha opened her eyes. She laid their almost motionless, gazing off at the ceiling until shifting her eyes around the room, eventually making eye contact with her husband. "What are you doing," Samantha managed to ask through a gasp, now aware of his stare. Simply taking in your beauty, and doing so in and with great gratitude. You being my wife and that you are here with me is truly a blessing. For so many mornings the reality I now live and possess, was only a dismal desire of a dream. Daily, I thought about you in some way, to some degree. Samantha, I dreamed about you nightly. I love you, I always have and I am so sorry, if that was ever a question to you or our family and   friends.   I

apologize if ever there was a time that my love for you did not show, or was not obvious and daily apparent. Life without you was horrible! Outside of what the Lord decides to do, when he decides to do it, I never want us to live apart again. I need every bit of, "what and who," you were meant to be, to and for Grae and me.

Really Guy, just stop! You are going to make me...before Samantha could head them off warm trails of tears made their way down the side of her face. See, you gonna make me cry like this first thing this morning? She managed to speak. Yelp! Guy firmly answered. No more assuming, and less taking things, people, for granted. If I tell you, then I know that you know, so I am telling you, you mean so much to me, you are like the air that I breathe, the wind in my sail, the ink in my pen. Outside of God, You are one of my daily necessities. I mean you, water, and food are like neck and neck he chuckled, wanting to see her smile. I need you, I want you, I like, love and appreciate you. Forever, will I cherish you Samantha, forever!

Awe, come her baby, Samantha spoke reaching out to her husband. She cradled him as close as she could to her heart. Listen, to me, you are every bit of my man, my guy. Until God says something different, now that I am here, right here, with you and Grae is where I am going to be. "I so love and appreciate you to Guy Shepherd," Samantha shared. They comforted each other with a warm embrace, and by now were both in silent tears.

Grace Sees and Extends Grace

It had been some time since that unexpected, harsh but honest revealing of a reality check, and since that evening, Grace had learned to view Stewart with a deeper genuine level of compassion. Just as he had proven to be, many years ago, he was still exactly, who and what, God intended for him to be in her life, that which she needed him to be. No longer did the mentioning of his name or the thought of him wipe away her smile or prompt an immediate frown or scour. With fasting, much prayer, and some long overdue dissecting of self, the blinders had been removed. Grace had been delivered from mere surface words and acts. Though it took some doing, her desire and determination to regain Stewart's trust, restore his confidence that she could and would, handle and properly take care of the children without his supervision, was at hand. It helped shift her focus, along with some other things as well. She had finally learned to simply, be. Something quite simple yet very complex for Grace, but in doing so, those natural, innate ways, words and actions kicked in, almost like operating on autopilot. "God you were, and still is, a very present and patient God, um."

"Hello Kathy answered." Hi, Kathy hold on for a second, I want to get Samantha on the line to. Grace informed. "Sure Kathy answered." Okay, Kathy, I am back hopefully she will pick up. Grace advised.

Well if it isn't Gracefully-Grace, hi Grace you still my friend? Samantha jokingly asked in her greeting. True to form Kathy laughed, understanding where Samantha was coming from. Now that is funny because Grace will skip out on you for like a week with no word, no text; not even a smoke signal, during the time when she is not friends with you. I mean if it were not for Stewart a few times in the past, I would have lost touch with a sistah. Kathy shared. Oh, wow, really Kathy. Girl, hush it up! Besides this is my call, so I get first dibs on the topic. Grace replied pulling the conversation back in her court. Ladies, now that we have gotten the greetings out of the way, I have a question for you two, which one of you are up for twin duty tonight? Grace asked. Tonight Grace that is a short notice, and as of what time because it will be late afternoon before I could be in route to pick them up. I also have a final venue viewing for a wedding tomorrow at 3p, so any time after that is questionable. Kathy answered. Grace, I would love to do it. Should we come pick them up, or will you bring them over on your way out? Samantha asked. Hold on ladies, Grace requested. Wait, is that it for me Grace, my client just pulled up, Kathy kindly interrupted. Sure, "go wow your client" girl. Grace answered. I love you ladies, and Grace I will do my best, Kathy concluded with a chuckle. We love you to!

Okay Samantha, I have not gotten that far yet. I just know that I have to seize the, "now," and do what I can to romance my husband in his love language, starting this evening. Right now, I am not sure on the how and what, only the when. Grace answered. I tell you what, Samantha suggested it is almost time for Grae to come home, once she arrive she and I will head over to your place. Go ahead and see what else you come up with, and once we get there, we will go from there. Thank you girl, I so love and appreciate you. I will see you two soon. Drive safely. Grace spoke before the call ended.

Once Grae arrived, she and Samantha headed for the car. So Grae, guess where we are going, Samantha playfully asked. Um, I don't know mommy, to the store. No, guess again. To daddy's office, Grae continued. No, one more guess, Samantha encouraged. Um, to the park, Grae offered. No, we are going over to Grace and Stewart's house. We get to see Grace and the twins, and guess what else? What Grae asked? The Twins will be coming home with us tonight! Oh, wow, really? Grae replied. They are so cute; I saw them at the cookout. Yes, really Grae, Samantha answered. Um, and now that I say it aloud, I am both excited and a little nervous. Well was daddy excited to, when you told him? Grae asked. Umm, such an interesting question Grae, Samantha replied. Why mommy, Grae enquired? "Because, though mommy knows that she should have; mommy did not run it by your dad first." Oh, you may want to call him first mommy,

Grae responded. Yeah, but I have already told Grace that they could come home with you and I. Oh wow; even then, I did not mention your dad. Um, okay let me pull over and give him a quick call. "Guy Shepherd speaking how may I help you? By saying yes, to the Adam twins sleeping over tonight, Samantha answered in her greeting. "Excuse me, what did you say, who is this?" Guy replied. Guy are you playing with me, this is Samantha, your wife! No, sweetie there was a burst of noise at the exact moment you began to speak. Guy answered. Well is it okay for the Adam twins to overnight with us tonight? Samantha asked. "Okay, so we are keeping the Adam twins tonight, is that what we are saying here?" Shh, it is a surprise, which is why it is such a late notice. Please tell me that Stewart is nowhere near you Samantha replied. No, not at the moment, Guy answered. Good, Samantha replied. So, is it okay? She asked again. Yes, sweetie it is okay. Do I need to do anything, or get anything, Guy asked. No, just come directly home because I am sure that Grae and I will need your help, and come with your game face on for two little ones because I never really raised a baby. I love you we will see you when you get home, Samantha spoke before the call ended. "Nor have I," Guy softly reminded himself.

Hey Guy, how are we looking for the rest of the day, I just got a call from Grace, for some reason she wants to know the earliest that I can get home this evening. I figured I would check in with you and Kevin before I gave her an answer. Stewart spoke as he entered Guys office. Well, let me think Guy answered in a slight delay, still thinking about having the twins for the night. Um, you know I feel good about the day's work thus far. I believe we will be fine until tomorrow. You go, go ahead and wrap up whatever you have going on and we will plug back in tomorrow. Guy encouraged. Okay then, great. I will give you a ring before I actually head out. Stewart spoke before leaving Guy's office.

Grace Displays Appreciation

Samantha and Grae had made it to Graces and were instrumental in helping Grace put her finishing touches, on a uniquely arranged, special evening, one that she created for only Stewart. Grace prepared a simple three-course meal for the two of them to return home to, and used the remaining time to ready herself for his home arrival. Though a little uneasy, she was ready. Ready, to once again, be truly transparent, open up, and confess, genuinely and sincerely apologizing. To extend and receive forgiveness as needed. This evening was about simply appreciating and loving her husband, openly. She had never truly stopped appreciating and loving him, but this fact just managed to, somehow get lost or rather buried under her misplaced attention and focus. Wow, ladies, look at this you two did a top-notch job! Thank you so much for your help and thank you for taking the little ones home with you. I promise you they will be a joy, and I believe that I have packed absolutely everything you will need, down to instructions, Grace ended in excitement.

The Shepherd family had quite an eventful evening. Both Samantha and Guy where amazed at how much they actually knew and knew how to do. They were pleased to learn some of the things they had never thought about when caring for small children. Grae had spoiled them because for the most part she was now a self-contained child. Wow, how long do you think those two will sleep? Guy asked Samantha as he crawled into bed. I do not know but I pray that it is on through the night, Samantha answered with a chuckle. Samantha, let me ask you something, is Grae going to be it for us? I mean, whatever you say, that is what it will be and I believe I can be happy with that, especially since it is a countless blessing now, to have you and Grae here and a part of my life. However, after tonight, I was able to see some of the things we missed, at least some of the things that I missed when Grae was born. I am not complaining in any way; however, after tonight with the twins, I do not know, I just feel some kind of way. That is all. You know what, I love and appreciate this time, my family now, and that is good enough. Time will tell. Good night Sam, I love you Guy offered as he sweetly kissed his wife on her shoulder, before nestling into a comfortable spot. Um, Samantha had remained silent, not because she opposed the topic, but because sadly and embarrassingly, though she and Grae went home to the same address, before moving here with Guy, Samantha could remember very little, rather close to nothing, about bringing Grae home and most of the years prior to now, and they had called the same place home. She finally made herself comfortable, but thanks to her restless thoughts, it was sometime before she went to sleep.

Soon enough, it was morning, and Samantha was still tired. What came first, the awakening voices of the little ones or the peeping sun now brightening up the room? Well now it really didn't matter, regardless of the answer, Samantha had to get up and check on her little overnight guest. "Okay little voices, Sammie hears you," she playfully spoke.

This not only acknowledged their cry, but it also encouraged her to get up out of bed. No, no, no Sam, you relax Guy spoke. Yeah mommy, we got this, Grae confirmed.

What? What do you know about babies? Samantha asked Guy and Grae. And what are you doing up Grae? Samantha concluded. The baby woke me up Grae answered. Oh I apologize baby, were they loud? How long had they been exercising there little vocals? Not long Grae answered. I must have been in a deep sleep then because I just noticed their voices Samantha replied. So did I mommy. Well, Grae if you just noticed their voices, and they just woke you, how did you get here so fast? Well do not be mad but when I got up for the bathroom I looked in on them and kind of fell asleep here on the floor while watching them sleep. Yeah she beat me to them Guy chimed in. I actually laid here watching for a few as Grae comforted them. When their voices picked up, I figured I should get up and help Grae take them to another room and attend to them, while you rest. So again, relax baby, Grae and I got this Guy spoke as he grabbed both babies, having Grae grabbed the baby bag, before they headed down the hall.

Though Samantha had mixed feelings about Guy and Grae being on baby duty, it had been a long night for her and before she could convenience her body to get up, she was overtaken by sleep. It seemed that time had simply melted away the and if it wasn't for her ringing telephone, the melting would have continued. "Hello," Samantha relaxingly answered through a stretch. "Um, girl where are my babies because sounds like you are asleep," Grace inquired in her greeting, totally omitting her true, hello. Girl please, we got the Midas touch in this house, everyone is relaxing over here in this camp. Forgive me God; Samantha mouthed looking upward relaxing she had no earthly idea the status of Grace's children. Especially since Grace's telephone cal woke her. So how was your night, Samantha asked filling the space before Grace could question her any further about the children. Grace shared a little about the evening, but soon looped back to the children in conversation. If it is fine with you and Guy, we would like to come for the children within the hour. Grace informed, ready to see her babies. Sure Samantha managed to encourage. We will see you within the hour.

"Guy, Guy where are you!" Samantha called out, almost frantically as she left the bedroom. "Shush." Guy softly responded as he headed toward his wife. The children are resting, what is it? Guy asked. Where, where are they resting because momma bear is on her way? Samantha asked, still a little elevated in her voice. Look, come see for yourself Guy offered, as he lead Samantha to where they all were resting. After she actually saw them, Samantha felt a lot better.

Whew, Grace just called; she and Stewart will be here within the hour to pick up the children. Moreover, why did you let me sleep so long, especially when I told Grace I would look after the children? Samantha asked. Are you serious Samantha, I doubt that you got any sleep at all with the way you tossed throughout the entire night. Well how would you know Guy, you were out like a light almost as soon as your head hit the pillows Samantha replied. Yeah, but the one time that I got up you were restless, I even watched you a little and decided to pray for you instead of completely waking you to ask if you were okay. So please, you needed that time of rest, that is why I let you sleep. Guy answered.

So you prayed for me, Samantha asked. Yes, I prayed for you. Guy answered. So tell me what did you pray, preacher. Samantha jokingly asked. Wait a minute now, "preacher," I would not go that far, but preachers are not the only ones that know how to pray. "Um hum, let me find out, sounds to me that you are trying to joke me." Guy replied with a chuckle. "That's fine though, either way I do believe that it helped because eventually you found a place of peace." Guy concluded. Okay Guy, you are right. "We still good, we ain't gonna fall out over that are we?" Samantha jokingly spoke with a smile. Wait, really Sam? Guy asked. No, seriously, Samantha replied with a straight face. Well okay, since you are taking it there, nope after all I have been through to be living out this moment with my family, it would take two life times for that to happen, but let's not purposely test it though, okay. Guy answered sealing it with a kiss. Humph sure, I agree but, that is something my mom use to say and it seemed like a good place to drop it.

Okay, all jokes aside. Please forgive me, and thank you for praying over me. May I ask what you prayed? "I asked God, to ease your mind, to settle your thoughts and to give you rest and peace, allowing you to sleep comfortable for the remaining of the night." Gheez, Guy spoke turning to walk away. Oh no, not like that you won't, Samantha spoke as she quickly hooked her arm around her husband's arm. No walking away Guy.

Okay Guy, look at me, listen and please hear me well. I asked, not to question you, but I asked because it truly was only a question. I am grateful for your prayers baby because I need them. I cherish you, I respect and love you Guy Shepherd and it was not, nor will it ever be my intent to make light of, or tease you, especially if it is a sensitive spot for you. Okay, you do hear me, right? I did tell you that I love you right; Samantha spoke as a reminder as she embraced her husband. Stop playing; you are cutting off my breath holding me like this. Guy gasped. Wow, am I now? Well good, I like hearing that, "I take your breath away". Samantha playfully spoke in laughter as she sweetly loosened her grip. Yes, sometimes you do Guy chuckled as he quickly kissed his wife before excusing himself to go get dressed. "Gotta get dressed, no telling how long it will be before Grace is knocking on our front door to claim her babies."

Guy and Grae, greeted Grace and Stewart at the door, but soon after Samantha joined in. The two families spent a little bounding time, but afterwards Grace and Stewart were loading up and on their way.

Life At K3 Horizons

It had been less than 48 hours since the heavy hitting blow for one of their own, and the last person the team at K-3 Horizons were expecting to see was Micci. She figured if she arrived early enough, her office presence could go unnoticed, and with it being the hectic morning that it was she presumed right, at least for a time.

A few hours into the day a few of the team members were checking in, dropping off or picking up a few work orders, and other things when they noticed Micci reviewing some blueprints. Seeing her at work moved them to many different emotions, they were tossed up between being surprised, shocked and intimidated as to how to approach her, some moved close, placing a compassionate touch upon her shoulder, while others extended a verbal apology. Having a few early appointments it was a lot later than usual when Kolin arrived. Nevertheless, when he did, the shock of seeing Micci at the office would not allow him to walk by her without offering, at best, some clicheic greeting. Kolin really did not trust himself to say the right thing at this moment, but he knew that he had to say something. In a voice more elevated than even he initially realized, Hey Micci, good to see you, grab that last sign-on file and walk with me will you. It took Micci a few moments but eventually Micci grabbed the file and accompanied Kolin. Once they reached a more discreet place, Kolin managed to say what was really on his mind.

"Micci," Kolin softly exclaimed. What, Micci asked. "What are you doing and why are you here at work?" Surprised and caught off guard, by Kolin's question the best Micci could manage at the moment, was an embarrassed, sorrowful glance. Stunned by his question, for a few seconds, Micci stood motionless with her mouth slightly open. Of all people to be asking these questions, Kolin was the last she would have expected of doing so. "Listen, you cannot pull a rug over something like this right now, I mean this is big Micci. This is a change that you will see or notice in some degree for the rest of your life. You need to know and understand exactly what it is that you are feeling and thinking so that it may be addressed properly. Now tell me absolutely everything I need to know - about this last sign-on because at least for the next two weeks, I will be your eyes, ears and mouth piece, and don't you worry I will operate as you, keeping you updated and in the know. You can also rest easy know that every dollar and cent of any incoming revenue that it generates will go to its rightful place. I would never shortchange you. Kolin suggestively instructed. Though grateful for the gracious offer, Micci firmly yet politely declined. No Micci, you do not understand. This is not an option. Let me borrow your cell phone for a moment. Why Micci asked as she handed over her phone. You will see soon enough. Kolin answer as he located the telephone number for Micci's mother. "Hello," Micci's mother answered. "Ah, yes. Hello ma'am my name is Kolin, one of the team members with your daughter Micci, her at K-3 Horizon how are you doing today. Ma'am I am standing her with Micci and though she does not yet realize it, she desperately needs somewhere to go for a week or two. Is this something that you can accommodate her with?" Kolin asked.

By now, Micci was quite vocal, so much so that even her mother could hear her. Kolin completed his call with Micci's mom then handed her the phone." Give me that!" "Momma, Hello?" She already hung up. She said to tell you that she would see you when you get there, this evening. By now with an elevated voice, it was obviously that Micci felt Kolin was overstepping his boundaries as a business partner. Right now, I am willing to risk you being angry with me for a few hours or possibly a few days because I know firsthand what this time a way will save you from. I have the opportunity to spare you from what I went through and that is exactly what this is all about. If you are going to learn what I learned, I rather you not learn it the way that I learned it. I now know that someone should have said more to me when my wife died. Now are you going to bring me up to date on this file before you leave or once you get to mom's house, because you are going, if it means that a group of us has to drive you ourselves!

After a short moment of awkward silence and a few weighty sighs, Micci open the file, pulled out a pen and the file briefing began. She told him everything she could possibly think of, and made a few notes on some specific pages before handing over the file. Okay the company will provide you a ticket so expect a confirmation call from our travel consultant. Otherwise, I want you to ignore you cell phone, better yet, turn your cell phone off. I mean that and when you get to your mom's house, you call this number. This is my mother's cell phone number; she will be expecting to hear from you once you arrive. Kolin advised. Okay, but shouldn't I give the number to you, Micci asked. Nope. This way when someone asks or demands to speak to you, I can honestly say that you are on a two-week hiatus and the only contact number that I have is the same cell phone number that they more than likely have, and besides, unless it is an absolute emergency do not expect to hear from anyone here at K-3. Please Micci, take this time to detach, release, unload and renew. I promise you, that by the time you get to the end of this two-week period, you will be wondering where the time went. Besides, it will take you about three or four days to embrace the fact that you are releasing yourself from work obligations, allowing yourself a little time off. Kolin, may I be honest with you? Micci asked. Sure, go ahead Kolin encouraged. Well my true thoughts are, "how is he going to tell me to do something that he didn't do himself?" Fare enough, Kolin replied. The answer to that is, because I found out the long and hard way, that someone should have said the same things to me, or at least something similar. Okay, to be fare maybe they did, no scratch that, my family did but by that time, I was not hearing a whole lot. After my wife died, to some extent I even had a deaf ear to the cry of my own child on some days.

In my case, it could be that those around me was too understanding, giving me too much space and time, granting me room to escape and proving to be a little too late by the time they began to say what needed to be said I had gravitated to a different place. It was a very unhealthy place, and daily it silently drained my passion for life. Creating a lot more work for me, and those who were brave enough to approach me to address it. Besides, I have an idea of where you are right now, and where you do not want to go. Trust me Micci just slip away. Go and allow moms to nurture and love on you as only she can. Kolin concluded. With tears standing in her eyes, her silence confirmed all that Kolin need to know. I tell you what, crybaby, I am going to head back inside, you get yourself together, even if it is only long enough for you can walk down that hallway, grab your things, "not work stuff," and get out of here. He gave Micci a friendly nudge with his elbow as he walked off. "Hey Micci, you're gonna go through a range of thoughts and emotions, you may even become a little envious of someone who appears to have all that you feel that you have lost, and that's okay for a time, but the important thing is you have to know that you cannot allow yourself to feel justified in parking there. Do not open that door, it is a scary dark place, and there is only room for one.

Thank you Kolin, thank you so much, Micci responded. Thank my mom, when I was or was not listening, my mom always knew exactly what to say, even when she didn't say a word. I believe that you are going to pull through this Micci; I believe that you are going to be okay, but most importantly, you have to know and believe it for yourself in order for it to happen. Kolin shared in his final comments as he walked off.

Micci took a few minutes before heading back inside. She not only heard him, but she was listening too. She knew Kolin was right, and now feeling just a little less weighted, she was beginning to appreciate the idea of going to be with her mom.

Hey mom, I am calling to inform you to expect a call from one of K-3 Horizons Contractors. Her husband did not make home from the job site last week, after a horrible work site accident claimed his life. Oh wow, that's tragic she gasped. Yeah, I agree, Kolin replied. She will be going away so she will be calling us to confirm her safe arrival. Okay, mom confirmed. Okay, still have a few things going on so I am going to get back to work, love you, he concluded.

Just as Kolin was wrapping up his short call Micci walked in and handed him her current open files. Thank you Kolin, I will call Sarah once I reach my mother's house, Micci shared. You are welcome, please be sure to do all that you can to enjoy and appreciate this time home with mom. I know for me, my mom helped make a big difference in the midst of my rough patch. Safe travels, Kolin encouraged. Thanks. Wait a minute, Kolin do you mind accompanying me to the elevator, I have quick question, Micci requested. Sure, I am headed that way, so what is the question, Kolin asked. Well just how much did this last minute travel arrangement cost me? Not a dime, Kolin replied. Now go heal.

On The Same Page

Though it had taken a lot of work, and they recognized they had even more work to do, both Stewart and Grace were finally reading from the same book, and on the best of their days, from the same page. Their marriage view did not look as it did before bringing home the twins, but at least they were on track to reaching that view once again, if not exceeding that. Stewart was so glad that God helped him to plant his feet, and stick and stay, and not give in to some of his selfish thoughts. He was grateful, to once again, have his wife's listening ear, and the sound of her true voice, um her voice; he lingered for a moment in thought. "Care to share," his guest asked as he entered. "Excuse me, what was that?' Stewart asked as he cleared his throat. Well I can only guess, but the look on your face a moment ago suggested that you were in a sweet spot, Stewart's guest answered. A "sweet-spot?" Stewart spoke with laughter, what is a sweet spot? He continued. Well sir, okay you are married right? His guest inquired. "Why, yes I am." Stewart answered. Okay, so wifey is all in your headspace right now isn't she? His guest continued. "Go on," Stewart encouraged with a chuckle. Well either she did or said something recently and just now, while you were in a quite still spot of the day, your mind chose to take you there, to your "sweet-spot." Stewart's guest concluded. Well yes, you nailed it. I was definitely in a "sweet-spot," as you call it.

Okay, enough of that what brings you by, what do we have going on today?

LORD Help Us

In the past few months, the family had grown more concerned for Junior, but the problem was, they did not know who to look to or where to take those concerns. Years ago, he along, with his family had learned of his diabetic medical issue, but from what they all could tell, he had lost most of the necessary weight, and it appeared that he was doing a fine job of living as a diabetic. They were all encouraged because he appeared to be making right and healthy choices.

Sarah wanted to better appreciate and relate to her brother, but over the course of time, she had grown disappointed with him for not living up to her expectations and to his "name sake". He was the second born son, but he was the one that wore the name of their dad. He was gifted and talented in so many ways yet, in her opinion living below and so short of his giftedness. In recent years, her personal frustration and disappointment of her brother had grown. It was not a secret to the one in which it mattered to the most, sadly, her brother Junior was well aware however, Sarah had no clue. Unfortunately, it would be much later before Sarah would gain knowledge and revelation of this fact.

Today with the thought of him weighting so heavily on her mind, Sarah began to talk to God about him. "Okay, God is something going on with Junior, why am I experiencing these feeling for him, and why am I having these dreams? I don't know what it is God, and I do not have to know, but Lord whatever, wherever his need is, "be it of; and or, for" You, please fulfill it. Watch over him, take care of him according to his need, he and Kerry both, for that matter. Help us to L.T.B. to simply, "Love Them Back," back to a place of spiritual, physical, mental and emotional balance, security, peace and health. Help us to care for them from a place of genuine compassion without judgment." Completing her verbal prayer, Sarah sat a little longer in silent prayerful thought, still experiencing a lingering, deep concern for her brothers.

The Yesterday, Today, And, "Never Promised" Tomorrow ~ Time

After about eight years of his health struggle, Sarah's family had gained knowledge of some of his unhealthy choices and the family was concern these choices could prove to be harmful for her brother Junior. Now knowing what they were fighting against, they searched the internet and made telephone calls, to make arrangements to position him for the assistance they thought he needed. They were hopeful that he could, and would totally, be restored to health, and their prayers along with this knowledge made for a more peaceful nights' sleep, especially for their mother.

Two weeks before the big appointment, Junior became dehydrated, later having to be admitted into the hospital. Because of this, the appointment would have to be put off for another time. He ended up being in and out the hospital, at least two more times before it appeared that things were turning around, and headed back to some sense of normalcy.

Chapter Six

Sarah Considered Surprising Her Brother

A few months had passed since her brothers spell of in and out of the hospital. Sarah thought about it a few weeks ago, but now she had actually completed the thought and was ready to put it into action. With another Friday here on hand, she would surprise him, showing up with dinner and a movie. A little hangout time with her brother had been heavy on her mind for some time.

Life, "as it always does," was making its rounds, and this morning it showed up at Sarah's front door. After many unsuccessful telephone calls, and after a failed attempted entry, just before six in the morning, there was a frantic knock on her door. Sarah sprang out of bed making haste downstairs.

"Who is it", she called out as she moved closer to remove the safety chain. When she looked out of the pep-hole, she could see that it was her younger sister T'wan. Sarah opened the door, and instantly, she knew that something was not right. With puffy eyes and a reddish face from excessive crying, her sister entered the house.

"Man, what is wrong with your phone?" she push out as she flopped down to the couch with a sorrowful sigh. "I have been trying to call you for the last hour almost. Sarah, he is gone. He's gone on away from this world." T'wan managed to speak through continual tears. Both motion and emotionless, Sarah gave no response. It took a few moments for her to completely, catch up to the moment. "What are you talking about?" she finally asked. "Sarah, Junior, he's gone. He is no longer with us. He is no longer among the living," her sister sobbingly answered. "I kept trying to call you, Kerry been calling me all morning. Kerry wanted to know where we were, he kept calling to tell me that we needed to hurry up and get there. He and momma were on their way to the hospital. When they got there, though his body was still warm, he was gone. Junior was gone." Wait a minute; Sarah finally spoke, so he is dead. You are telling me that, Junior is dead. Though she had more questions, Sarah finally took a seat on a couch, across from her sister and they both set in verbal silence for a few seconds.

Okay, what happened, what do you know, what did they tell you once they got there? For some time, she and her younger sister T'wan set there talking through the shocking news of the death of their, 46 year old brother. In that moment, they were there for each other the best that they knew to be.

They both knew death had no age restrictions, but he died younger than their dad who had died unexpectedly, in 1996, at the age of 55, it was just twelve days short, of what would have been his 56th birthday. "Why Lord, why?" She voiced, not necessarily asking the question.

This was a lot to take in, and though Juniors health was not the best, his was a condition; they all thought he could live through, and with. All day every day, somewhere in this world people from all walks-of-life, were doing just that. So why not here, and why not with, and for her brother she wondered? Ump, so many unanswered questions she pondered.

After receiving the "live and in person", news of her brothers' death, she had only spent a few moments in silence before grabbing her cell phone to get the word out. Now, moving past her initial shock, Sarah first began by contacting her employer. After leaving the voicemail with her employer, Sarah emotionally and mentally squared her shoulders and kicked into that, "okay, what do we need to do mode," showing little to no emotion. She then found it easier to inform all others by sending a mass text. It was the quickest way she knew to move the news along to multiple people at once, so while her little sister continue to release her emotions, that is exactly what Sarah did. Once she received the arrangement updates for the funeral, Sarah sent another mass text, with an update of the forthcoming arrangements.

Kerry, there oldest brother, and her parents first born son, he along with her older sister, her parents first born girl", were in town, and at home with mom, assisting with the funeral arrangements. In what seemed to be a short amount of time, they managed to get mostly everything taken care of.

One of the last things to do was to shop for a suit for Junior to be buried in. The second born child, George Lee McNair, Jr., ump.

Kerry volunteered to try on the suit, ensuring a perfect fit. He along with Lina where doing all that they could to assist mom but it was hard, and now, with them in route to shop for Junior's last suit, made it that much more real and a lot harder by the second.

Saying Goodbye

Sarah and T'wan had a few things to wrap up at home before packing up for their 120 minute, 125-mile drive. Wow, final funeral preparations, I know that such is life, but this feels wrong. A forever farewell, to her 46-year-old brother was just a matter of hours away. "Ump", in the breath of a sigh, was the best she could offer at the moment as she continue to take it all in and try to, properly embrace for her family's reality.

It was not evident yet, but soon, there would be, a much needed release. Sarah by nature was an adapter, a responder quite far from being a reactor. Sarah and T'wan finally made it to their mom's house but it was not without event. Being the designated

134

driver, Sarah had a few incidents that caught her off guard. They both startled her so much, that it caused her armpits to itch, each time. Of course, as one may suspect, each time her sister T'wan was completely distracted missing both unfoldings.

First, it was a deer, and then, it was a dog, and upon both sightings Sarah released a firm, "JESUS," before bring the vehicle back into alignment of her traveling lane after avoiding possible contact. Each time, T'wan was like, "ump, are you okay? Do you need me to drive, because I am not seeing any of this stuff that you are supposed to be seeing?" I promise you, it is not just me; I keep getting these surprises, and seeing stuff on the edge of the road headed in our direction, which of course made me swerve and call out. First, it was a deer, and then it was a dog. I am telling you the truth mannn, it really was!

Now at mom's house, Sarah was the first to get out of the vehicle and enter the house. When unlocking, and opening the door, a seemingly wave of questions were released as she barely got one foot across the threshold of the doorway. "There they go, "how... what..., how do you think...?" the questions continued.

Sarah had entered the house through the lower level seating area, which is where her, older brother, sister, mother and one of the funeral home representatives had assembled to finish up the last remaining details regarding Junior's funeral.

The ambush of questions, on the heels of the drive home was a lot to balance yet Sarah being Sarah, firmly yet politely, requested a few moments to collect her thoughts as she advised she would have to come back to the questions hurled at her upon her entry. "Um, you are gonna have to give me a minute", Sarah replied as she pressed through the thickness in the air because of the reason for this gathering.

Her greeting and entrance were both, weighty and thick, and Sarah had yet to realize how personally challenging it was, having to be gathered with the rest of her family for this reason. Before she could completely move away from the door, her younger sister had caught up, and was now standing behind her. Like Sarah, and barely a step inside the door, those already seated where in repeat mode, firing off the same questions for T'wan, and like Sarah, she too felt ambushed having no, readily available answers. When having the same lineup of questions hurled at her, "Y'all are gonna have to give me a minute" T'wan extended in rapid response.

After having a moment to detach from the drive, Sarah and T'wan were as ready as they were going to be to assist in any way they could to help close out the remaining funeral arrangements. Things began calmly, moving along smoothly until a question, along with a suggestion, surrounding the eulogy, and personal comments was both spoken and stated, "who do we asked to carry out what?" Mom stood quietly at the kitchen sink finishing up the dishes while her remaining four children stood around the end of the bar, attempting to figure it out and come to a place of decision so the funeral home representative could be on his way. Before this last need could be finished, the calm and smooth chatter had turned into, the firing of heated, personal, and elevated words with the voice of Sarah and her oldest brother, the first born, verbally going back and forth in their disagreements.

Finally hearing one of his sisters, and seeing the conversation getting out of hand, Sarah's brother extended his arms, attempting, offering along with a verbal apology, to hug Sarah, as he reminded her that he loved her, but it was a little too late for Sarah. Right now she wanted him nowhere near her, she merely heard his apology, receiving and embracing not, his hug. So viewing this as rejection and unchristian like, during an already heavy and painful time, once again her brother Kerry became quite vocal in sharing his unwanted opinion of Sarah with her.

Now that they were getting absolutely nowhere, Lina, Sarah's older sister and T'wan, her youngest sister chimed in trying to be the voices of reason, and to pull Sarah and Kerry back in so they could, not only complete this last task, but also make it possible for the representative from the funeral home, to be on his way. But there attempts and efforts were fruitless, and now with her voice, as strong as it had, more than likely ever been in her entire life, Sarah's verbal communication turned into a loud wailing of an outcry that silenced the room.

This was the first time Sarah's mom had ever silently stood by while her children where fussing. Yet for some time, there she quietly stood at the kitchen sink in the midst of their booming voices.

Having no more fuss left, Sarah's fuss had now turned into a tearful and prayerful language, both of Sarah's sisters, as well as her brother surrounded her and huddled her in a long overdue, sibling group hug.

This was something that Sarah desperately needed, as she wailed and cried out, to a point of being weak. She was so weak that she could no longer stand. Her sister Lina noticed the need to support Sarah's weight just as her brother Kerry was telling her to stand up.

"Stand up, Sarah stand up before you fall" "Kerry, wait a minute, she can't, she can't stand up," Lina spoke. While Lina and Sarah's sister, T'wan slid a folding chair closer, Kerry directed Sarah's body to the chair, for her to seat down. After a time of obvious, "necessary brokenness", the siblings were back to a united front and were able to sign off on the remaining funeral arrangements, finally able to send the funeral representative on his way.

Though sadness and lost was in the air, from that moment on, a sweet beautiful blanket of comfort and peace hugged them each individually, exactly and specifically as they needed it, and it was felt throughout the entire process of both the wake and the funeral. Their family and friends showed up in large numbers. Special classmates of the deceased as well as of Kerry, Lina and T'wan filled the home, carport and driveway of their mother's home. Though Sarah's heart was warmed by the few friends from her past that made time to come and render support, there was one in particular that she just knew without a shadow of a doubt would, at some point be there for her and she was looking forward to seeing this individuals face.

Everything within her knew that she could count on this special friend, and upon this friend's arrival, then, she would not have to be strong anymore. This thought alone renewed her strength. For this was the one who knew the rhythm and beat of her heart, her strengths and weakness, her failures and her victories. The one she trusted her life to, and there was no question in her mind if this person would be there for her, the only question was, when? For without a doubt, and in a moment, they would show up and be front and center.

Though yet to make a personal appearance, this friend had been nursing her along with telephone calls from the moment of the receiving of the news. She was certain that, be it a few moments, before or after the wake, be it before, during or after the funeral, or waiting for her to return to town after wrapping things up from the funeral, "yes they will be here," she reminded herself.

Still resting in the peace of God, and the comfort of the fact that soon the arms of this trusted friend would come and comfort her, Sarah once again squared her shoulders, put on the face of strength, enabling her to endeavor the remaining responsibilities of the funeral.

When it became obvious that this trusted friend would not get there any time before the wake and funeral, more and more Sarah weakened in her strength and self-encouragement as she awaited her friend's arrival but in a matter of days she would head back home where there would be no eyes watching and no outside expectations of here. "Hold on Sarah, hold on," she softly sighed.

It had been about three days since the burial of Sarah's brother, and having made it back home, she knew it would not be much longer now. For throughout this whole ordeal, this friend had never stopped calling. To both Sarah and the trusted friend, it was evident that their presence was greatly needed and now, this was it. The "it," that it had been about all along, and though they spoke on the telephone, throughout it all, the truth had set in and she finally got it. "He's not coming," she silently informed herself. This trusted and needed friend, still had yet to arrive, and he was not going to show up anytime soon, or in the near future. "So he is just going to "not" come through for me after all? Wow. I am so, not believing this! Nah, believe Sarah. Believe it. "

At that moment, she stopped what she was doing to allow her mind to, play back most of the calls and conversations. She was so done. Sarah had enough and made a decision. She was done with allowing this friend to nurse her along with telephone calls. Especially when now, more than any time before, she needed their presence. Right now, as small as it may seem to some, it was big to Sarah, and what she wanted was a hug. She wanted the hug of this trusted and long time friend, but of all the times to be absent, this friend was not available now, in one of the weightiest times of her life. She gave herself a harsh reality check, "not only were you absent all this time, but you really are not coming," she disappointedly thought aloud of this friend.

Sarah at that moment turned the cell phone off. She chose to direct her attention to her sister Lina, whose flight would be leaving first thing in the morning and after gathering for such an event this served as a fresh reminder of the importance of life and family, which was as aromatic in the air, as the scent of fresh wet paint. These would be well lived out moments, and they were going to enjoy the few remaining hours as best they could.

Lina had noticed something different about Sarah but chose, not to mention it before now. Sarah was not the only one looking for and expecting to see this well trusted, long time friend, but Lina, along with some other family members were too. Once they had gathered, close family members asked Sarah a number of times, what time her friend would get there. They wanted to know where her friend was, some wondered if her friend even knew what was going on.

Now back at her own home, and with the friend not showing up before now, and with her still, processing her brother's unexpected death, just 5 months into his 46th year of life, Sarah was feeling some kind of way. Even with this being her reality, she would have to figure out a way to relationally, mentally and emotionally, "get up" and "do life." Moreover, that is exactly what she did, and she managed to do so with a firm, unwavering smile.

Delanda McNair

Chapter - Seven

It was the morning of her sister's return flight home and Sarah had mixed emotions. Though she really needed some alone time with her big sister, and she did not want her to leave, consciously, she did not want her sister to see her true state. How she was weaker than she had ever been in her life.

"So Sarah now that I am going back, what time will your friend get here? Her sister Lina asked. I am not sure, you know, with all of the talking that we have been doing, I never even asked where they were or exactly when they would get here, Sarah replied. "But they are coming though?" Lina asked. Again, I do not know the answer to that one either, girl I never directly, asked my friend if they were coming and I never actually asked him to come, Sarah answered. "Yeah, but he has to know that you needed him to be here, especially now that you are back home and all alone." I guess time will soon tell. Sarah managed to answer remaining calm and emotionless.

Her sister thought and believed she was strong and brave, and Sarah could show her nothing less than that. The sooner she could get her dropped off at the airport, the sooner Sarah could be by herself, drop her extremely tired weighted shoulders, and exhale. Moreover, that is exactly what she did, now at the airport, she helped to get her sister unloaded at curbside for check in, greeted her with a hug, love salutations and, bidding her safe travel and they were both off. Her sister walked through the sliding doors and Sarah blended into the flowing traffic and drove off.

For more reasons than one, silent tears escorted Sarah home, and decided to show up periodically throughout that incoming week.

Sarah Flooded With Emotion

It had been right at 4 months," man it is hard to believe that we are at the end of the month of July," Sarah silently thought. It had been a little over 4 months since the death of her 46-year-old brother and Sarah still was not the same. There was an underline "something" going on, yet as sure as she was about this underline "something," she lacked the same assurance as to "what" it was. Lacking any details or specifics, kept her from being able to address it so she could completely exhale, release, and move on so to speak. "Um, we will come back to this one"

The day began, and it was a new morning full of fresh blessings, though Sarah knew this to be true, she still found herself facing a little bit of emotional weightiness, as her mind took a short trip, back down memory lane. It had been more than 13 years ago, when she answered the telephone only to hear the cutting news of her father's death. On some days the reality of his permanent absence, was in some ways, as fresh as the day of that call all those years ago.

Embracing the sweet memories of her dad, reminded Sarah of how much she missed him, and how she still needed his voice, and conversation. Um, ever was he missed, she thought. Flashing thoughts of her dad's words of wisdom, his ways and actions danced around in her head while the thought of the recent burial of her 46 year old brother, filled any empty pockets of her mind.

"Okay, you have to get up, and move from this weighty place, Sarah encouraged herself. Guess I'll just log on, and see what's going on on social media." Shortly after logging on, a smile found its way to her face as she read a few celebratory and encouraging posts from the main screen.

Reading of good cheer, helped roll away some of her emotional heaviness. From there she pulled up specific pages of people she cared about, to somewhat reconnect with them and to get a glimpse of what they were up to. In doing so, one of the posting read: "Oh my goodness, I'm so excited my dad got married yesterday!" Sarah took great interest, because the young person responsible for this post was the daughter of her trusted friend, the one that never showed up in the midst of one of the times that she needed him the most.

Sarah was left, almost breathless after reading this post. It left her motionless for some time, and it took even more time for Sarah to completely, comprehend and accept the reality of what she had just read. "I have to be missing something," she thought aloud, which prompted her to search a little deeper, and with a few clicks of her computer keys she had her answers, and it was, "all true, and all confirmed".

Now, on top of already feeling emotionally weighted, she now felt a high level of anxiety too. Sarah deeply wanted, that which she felt painfully within the core of her heart, to **"not,"** be true. At that moment, it was the last thing that she needed. She sat quietly in disbelief, "how did this come to be, and how is it that this is the way that I find out," Sarah internalized.

Wow!

For about the space of an hour, if not two, Sarah was ambushed, so many emotions meet her in this moment. It seemed silence, was the best comfort she had to offer, or render to herself. Following the silence, came the internal self-check. After being brutally honest, and reminding herself, that they had stopped dating, that some time ago, they had removed the relationship title, and being that way for some time, now her main issue was, having to face the fact, of being betrayed by a friend. This was someone that she believed in, and someone that at one time she trusted with her life.

Well, "You Taught Me." Now I see why you kept me on the telephone instead of showing up in person, she thought aloud. He was engaged, and prepping for life with someone other than her. Um, all that talking he was doing to, and with me, as if, his time was his time, when the truth of the matter was that he was months away from saying "I Do." What kind of person does that? Man, I would have never thought or believed him to be this type of cowardly, thoughtless, selfish liar. "Um, never!"

There she sat, alone and by herself, in her bedroom sharing both her verbal and silent thoughts with God. Sarah finally released a much-needed sigh as she spoke, "okay Lord, I desperately need You to help me to truly and genuinely let go and let God on this one. I honestly desire and choose to, without a grudge or any bitterness, to let go and let God, casting no blame, and judging not. Whew!"

Well God, it is written; "no good thing will HE withhold from them that walk uprightly…," well simply put, I take it that he was not my good thing. For if, Your word reminds us, "the promises of the Lord are yea and Amen," I also take it, that he was not my promised man or mate. God I know, that You know the plans that You have for me, so if he wasn't a part of Your plans for me, then what were You waiting on to tell me, and how did I manage to miss, or rather ignore the signs?

Oh, but wait a minute, I guess that is what You was telling me, about seven years ago. Ump God, now you know in addition to being saved from others; sometimes, I just need to be saved from myself as well. Shoot, I want my investment in him back. Let Miss "new girl," cultivate him. Lol, okay I am being silly now, but for real though, while I am in this place of honest reflection, thank you for saving me from myself when necessary and those "obviously," not having my best interest at heart. Whew, ever do I need Your help with the way that You are answering this one. This is not an easy pill to swallow. God, I know it is a wrong thought to have, but right now, I kinda want someone else to hurt too. "Shoot! I'm just being honest Lord. You know that I am thinking it anyway." Ha ha ha.

Sarah made it through Saturday, and now it was Sunday morning, "Well, it's off to church we go, at least no one will notice my range of emotions there, ha ha ha", Sarah voiced in an attempt to press on and move beyond her disappointment and deep cutting hurt.

With a soft sigh of relief and the help of God, she did it. Sarah made it through Sunday morning service, and was now, back in her vehicle heading home. Sarah reminder herself that nothing catches God by surprise, that being a perfect God, He made no mistakes. She began to try to back track in her mind to see if she could put her hand on or figure out why God did not seal their relationship with His blessing by saying yes, by making all of their necessary points meet. "Ump" she sighed, scripture penned it. "His ways are not our way His thoughts are not our thoughts…" I am sure I could spend the rest of the week attempting with, in and of, my little human mind, to figure this one out, the results, are indeed just that, "the end results." Guess that is one more thing that I am going to need you to help me let go of please, and thank you Sir for all of your help. Well once again, I give it to you!

Sarah Gets Real

Weeks, then months unfolded and though Sarah greatly, and most importantly, missed her friend, which was one of few who knew her in some ways better than she knew herself, she managed, with God's, grace and help, to move, upward, onward and forward.

"Ump, if it could be chosen, of the three, I wonder what most people would choose; to endure, to go through and or to deal with; 1) a mental, 2) an emotional or 3) a physical trial or weight?" Just a thought God, I am so not asking to know or learn the answer firsthand. Feeling a combination of two of the three just positioned me, to entertain the thought for a second or two. Anyway, Lord even in this place and moment, I have to thank you, for it is no question, for You always know best. I just may need some time to catch up to the reality of that truth.

Still in the center of this "upward, onward and forward" point of view, and what, (or should we say, who), drove her to this place, of all that tried to flood her mind, "Lord I thank you," was Sarah's current response and offering. In response to the thought, and reality of the betrayal, hurt, as well as the possible, and justified, bitterness and anger, there was no better focal point for her. For even now, God was still a good God, and she could not forget the fact that He had actually given her direct and specific instruction about this man, which she received an "I, for Incomplete that is", for incompletely and disobediently, carrying out His command, all those years ago. Um, guess this is what I get, for choosing to play a role in the way that I did, smart self, "NOT" huh, Sarah jokingly teased herself.

"I choose to genuinely and completely, extend forgiveness releasing the possible binding effects of bitterness and anger. God not only do I want to expect and receive Your best, in and upon my life, and the life of those around about me, but I genuinely pray Your best in and upon both of their lives as well, as well as their union.

Forgive me for whatever negative role that I may have played in this situation or the events leading up to this point, or its outcome. I release, and extend self-forgiveness, and I welcome, embrace and receive Your grace, mercy and forgiveness for me. I choose to, allow it to be applied to and upon, every area and aspect of my heart, mind, body, soul and spirit. Mentally, emotionally, relationally, physically, psychologically, and econoMiccilly, in every way shape form and or fashion, to and upon, my entire being and existence, all people places and or things," Sarah laughed aloud. Okay God, I know that, that one was a little extra, but hey, right now, with all of what I am feeling and experiencing, I need to make sure all my bases are covered!

I just have to be in place and position, from here on to receive the promises and blessings that You have for my life and me. I do not know if I can survive any other way, and after "all" of this, I do not want to have to try to find out. I just need to know that I am walking, doing, speaking and thinking accordingly, that I am in alignment with You and Your word.

Better yet, Sarah thought a loud as she searched for the record feature on her cell phone," I gotta document this one". She decided to verbally release her prayer thoughts a loud, recording them as she boldly recited them believing, in and with great faith, that HIS best would so be seen and lived out in her life. This was the first but would not be the last of her audio prayer log. She would use them to make her very own little personal audio prayer book, and she was looking forward to revisiting them at the end of the year.

It was going to be an interesting way to reflect on the prayers prayed and spoken; and how HE answered them when closing out the current year, gearing up, and prepare for the incoming new one. Sarah gave it a title and decided now was a good time to be completely still and rest, and right now I say thank you for delivering, "Your best" in and upon my life. I receive it, so bring on the new! Goodnight.

Living From A Distance

Though undetected by Kolin, those close to him noticed how he used business and modern day affordability, to only "politically" aid in his escape from parenthood. On nights and weekends, when Kevin and Kathy were forced, "to say no", to being his babysitter, he would call on a professional service. Close family knew that he was avoiding "parent duty," it seemed that pick up and drop off, was what he had managed to skim it down to. Kevin and Kathy at times, wondered how often he actually made physical contact with his little one. They grew more and more concerned, and recently collaborated on what they could do, without pushing him to a deeper, colder place of denial. With recent concerns for Kaye and now growing concerns for Kolin, Kevin and Kathy had been praying a lot more in the past months. It is possible, that they had not prayed this much since Kathy's pregnancy, or the pregnancy of Grace Adam.

Though Kolin's little one was still rather young this was still a pivotal point in the little one's life and it was well past time for Kolin to be more active, and more hands on in it.

After much prayer and consideration, it was time for Kevin to talk to his brother, and he was going to make it a lot sooner than later.

It may have gone unnoticed to most, but Kolin had been both hearing and listening to the concerns, of those he cared about. The interesting thing, was that after all this time, he truly believed that he was okay. The fact that he had completely lost his smile, warmth, and becoming almost, "stoic" had totally escaped him. So privately, and very quietly, he sought to figure out a way to hear and see what his friends and love ones heard and saw. He endeavored to experience, "the him," those around him experienced. Kolin wanted to know what they were talking about, he wanted to see for himself. "How much could I have actually changed?" he softly spoke. Adjusting to the unexpected responsibilities of single parenting was a big thing, and for him an awkward hat to wear. With these being some of the thoughts fresh on his mind, his quiet "self study," began, and over the course of time he slowly saw and sometimes heard, some of what those around him saw and heard.

When he compared Kolin; the Kolin who'd mapped out his career plan by the age of 17 and totally living out his dream before the age of 20, to the Kolin today, he could honestly say everyone around him were onto something and a lot had changed about him. "Wow, why did I change so much, and when did it all happen?" Immediately, at the conclusion of that softly spoken question, memories of his son's birth and of his wife and her sudden death convene in his mind. However right now, it was a lot more than what he wanted to think about. This "self study" was the last thing he wanted to do. He grabbed his phone and made a few calls, what better time than now to respond to received messages and confirm a few appointments.

Sarah Wants Her Daddy

"Man, this is such a Daddy moment." Sarah softly spoke with a sigh as she embraced an unshakable overwhelming desire for his insight and input. It had been more than a decade now and still, his presence and conversation were as fresh and present in her surroundings, as the aroma of freshly baked pastries that could be smelled from blocks away. It was one of those moments, and right now, her memory was setting her up for an emotional ride. Ump, still to this day there were so many "him" discussions she lost the opportunity to have. Discussions that she could now only, "partially and one-sidedly", play out in her head. To say that she missed him, could only partially tell the story or express Sarah's feelings and her level of lost. Of all the thoughts, and life chapters that never got shared, the fact that she could never walk down the aisle with him at her side, and that her possible children, would never know him or build a bond and relationship with him, cut like a dull knife. That day long ago was the death of a number of things for Sarah.

Though thoughts and images of, recent marriage and baby announcements, along with prior attended weddings and celebratory showers, attempted to clutter her mind, Sarah smiled within. For in that moment, and the face of her singleness, she managed to encourage herself, "you are the God of love, not hate, of peace and balance, not confusion, and no good thing will you withhold from me...", ump, Sarah sighed. " Thank you Lord for keeping, and preserving me, and in advance, I am saying thank you, for my "GOD-u-factored" mate. From now until the delivery of "Your" appointed time, arrival, and well after, I now pray this prayer, over myself as well as my GOD-u-factured him." On that note, Sarah transitioned and moved on through the course of her day.

It had been a little over a year and for some time now Sarah had come to the reality that she needed to be more active in things that mattered, things that benefited someone other than herself, but what on earth, could that be. For months now, this had been a lingering question. Sarah prayed the soon receipt of an answer. As she sat staring off into the distance, at nothing in particular her telephone rang.

"Hello, Sarah answered. Well hello sis, this is Mother Glenda, how are you doing today?" It was the first lady of her church and Sarah felt honored to receive her call. "Hello Mother Glenda, I am well how are you doing?" "Honey I am the child of the All Mighty King, I am excellent!" "Okay now mother," Sarah, replied as they both shared a little laughter. So what exciting things do you have going on today? Sarah continued "Honey, so much so, that one set of hands and one set of feet could not get it all completed if I had four days to get it done," the mother answered honestly with laughter. Oh no Mother Glenda, you do know what happens when you burn the candle at both ends right, Sarah asked. Well I have an idea, Mother Glenda replied, but tell me what happens anyway. She continued in more laughter. Well, you become a puddle of wax twice, if not four times as fast. Sarah answer. Um, sounds like you need another set of hands and feet Sarah managed to finish in her laughter. I know that's right sis Sarah, thank you so much for offering sis. What time can you meet me here at the church, today or tomorrow, I have a few things that you may be able to assist me with." Still catching up to what had just happen, though sluggishly, Sarah managed to give her a time and shortly after the call end.

What in the world just happened, Sarah spoke aloud after the call ended. Wow, okay God I have no clue what it is, but whatever it is please help me to execute this mission with a true servants heart.

When Sarah, met Mother Glenda at the church, they chat just a few moments before Sarah received a description and explanation of the tasks she was to carry out. Sarah accepted the mission, advising mother Glenda that she would touch bases with her at the end of the day, to brief her on the unfolding.

First stop was the delivery of a box of clothing collected for one of the local shelters. Second stop was the post office to drop off a few cards to some sweet church members who had been a little under the weather. Sarah left the post office with two more stops to make one was lunch for a special elderly couple then not too many block away some kind of paperwork to a contracting company.

Everything unfolded smoothly until her third stop. It was so hard to find a place to end the conversation with the sweet couple that Sarah found herself running behind on time. Finally able to, politely excuse herself she made her way to the last drop off to deliver the envelope.

"Almost done, let's get this envelope delivered," she softly encouraged herself. Sarah found the building, parked, and made her way inside. Spending way more time than she expected with the meal delivery, Sarah was looking forward to this being a smooth, *in – and - out* delivery so she could head home. Now inside, her focus, at this point, was the envelope and the elevator.

Sarah was headed for the elevator when the attendant called out to her. "Ma'am, may I have you to step over here please." "Gladly," she answered. "Just sign in and we will point you in the right direction!"

Sarah informed the attendant who she was, but they were unable to locate her scheduled appointment. Apologetically, they informed her that they would need to get her expected party on the phone. Well, Sarah did not have a name, and being extremely late, by now she was a little frustrated. Being way too embarrassed to call Mother Glenda; Sarah asked if she could just leave the envelope at the desk. The attendant kindly explained how that was not an option, so he placed a call upstairs to see if he could get someone to come down from the fourth floor and receive the envelope from her. Sarah stood by while the call was made, the first call went straight to voicemail, but instead of leaving a voice message, the attendant simply ended the call and called right back. This time he was able to get someone to answer the line. After explaining the situation, someone agreed to come retrieve the envelope. Moments later, a K3 Horizons representative appeared to receive the envelope, after politely thanking Sarah they then turned to head back upstairs. Once upstairs, the envelope was placed in the "incoming mail" bin to be distributed by the office assistant with the other daily mail.

Kolin Gets Stood Up

Hello Mother Glenda did you forget about me today. Well hello to you sir what do you mean Mother Glenda asked. Well, wait a minute, Kolin requested. Let me check my personal calendar, maybe I missed something. "Oh my, please forgive me; it is not you at all. I know exactly what you are referring to. In all of my rearranging, I never call ahead to give you a forewarning." A forewarning, of what Kolin asked. "Well, haven't you received the envelope by now?" No and since it is not like you to be tardy I wanted to call and first make sure all is well with you and then find out just why you stood me up today Mother Glenda. Again, I must apologize, but just a second dear are you able to hold on for a few seconds one of my assistants are calling in, one second Kolin."

Hello, she answered. Mother Glenda this is Sarah, and I just need to give you a little update on the short to do list I was responsible for today. Everything went... hold on dear, wait a minute where are you, I am sitting in my car about to head home Sarah answered. Have you left K3 Horizons yet my dear, Mother Glenda asked. No but I am about to. No, I need you to go back. Tell me, what did Mr. K3 himself say when you handed him the envelope? Well nothing, Sarah answered. Okay wait a minute, let me backup. I am not sure, that it was Mr. K3 himself, that came downstairs to retrieve the envelope Sarah informed. You see..."your name was not in the appointment book so you never made it up stairs, I completely forgot to call ahead to inform them to expect you instead of me. Go back my dear I need you to go back and Mr. K3 himself will meet you downstairs. Run along dear we will catch up later." Oh my, hello. Mother Glenda spoke resuming her call with Kolin. Mother Glenda, are you avoiding me for some reason Kolin asked? Of course not my dear but listen take the envelope, and head down stairs I never made it to your building today but sent my assistant instead, the only thing is that I forgot to call ahead to advise you to expect her instead of me. Well, what is her name and I will call downstairs now, "no-no-no, never mind that", Mother Glenda interrupted, just get down there and meet her. Oh no, I need to go my dear but I will be in touch later. Her last words to Kolin were, goodbye for now," as she could be heard already going into another conversation in the distance. As Kolin cleared his office, in route to the stairs his stomach released a loud long growl. "I know I know I know, we will get something to eat in a bit, I want to eat too" he softly spoke as he allowed his hand to rest upon his stomach for a few seconds.

Before reaching the bottom of the steps, he noticed the look of an "unsure" woman as she stepped inside. "Hello," he spoke with confidence making direct eye contact. "I am willing to bet my lunch that you are the assistance that Mother Glenda instructed me to come downstairs and meet." Kolin spoke now having Sarah's full attention. "Ump, that's a partial truth. Her assistant, no however, she did send me over to first deliver, and now back to confirm the receipt of delivery of her envelope." Sarah answered. I see, Kolin replied. Tell me about this envelope. Well I stopped by earlier but when I was unable to make it past the guard at the front gate over there, he was kind enough to get someone from K-3 Horizons to come downstairs and retrieve it. Sarah replied.

"Ha ha ha, the guard at the front gate," I think that is my first time hearing that one. Kolin laughed in response. Well, the envelope never got to the person Mother Glenda intended it for, are you sure, it was given to a K-3 Horizon represented? Kolin asked.

Honestly, Sir, I am not sure. I do not know the name of the person it was intended. I did not even know the name of the company until I actually arrived to deliver the envelope in question. The same envelope I left behind with a man that came downstairs, only after the attendants' two failed telephone calls. Ump, so he had to call up twice, ump interesting Kolin replied.

Sir, I ask this respectfully, but why does it matter right now that the attendant called twice? Sarah asked. I personally, am more concerned with the fact that an envelope, that I was responsible for has yet to show up with the person that it was intended for, Sarah spoke. Okay, I guess you have a point, Kolin replied with a chuckle. Let us go over to the counter and call upstairs Kolin suggested.

Before they could step away from where they were standing Sarah's stomach released a loud long growl. So much so that before he knew it, Kolin commented. "Oh wow, you to huh," he spoke as he pointed, looking toward her stomach. Too embarrassed to speak, the best Sarah could offer were enlarged eye expressions in disbelief of what had just happened. I tell you what; Kolin began to speak with a chuckle. Are you hungry, let us grab something to eat? Now finally able to blink, Sarah lapped her eyes as she replied, "what, no you didn't, what did you just ask me" Sarah continued. "Oh my," why did that not come out the way I meant for it to Kolin spoke. Okay allow me to try to clean that one up.

I am about an hour late in eating. To be honest, the reason for that surprising and maybe out of order comment is that, just a few moments ago, as I was on my way to meet you my stomach released the exact same long and loud noise. It is just that no one else was around when it happened to me. So since it sounds like we could both use something to eat, and note I did not say that you were hungry, why don't we, just turn around, head out the door, and cross the street, and sit down to something good to eat? There how did I do with the clean up, Kolin asked?

Not too bad of a clean-up job, Sarah answer, but the answer is, no. What, excuse me, Kolin spoke, "No?" Why is your answer no, may I ask? Well I do not care if it is in the middle of the afternoon, I do not go to lunch with strangers. Sarah spoke firmly, yet ending with a quick and soft smirk.

Humph, Kolin sighed loudly as he headed for the door, while suggesting with the nod of his head that Sarah come along. She turned around and kept eye contact as he moved toward the door but she did not move. As Kolin stood in the doorway with the door, propped open for Sarah to come along, once again his stomach released a long loud growl. See, I told you Kolin spoke as he patted his stomach. Again, he gave a nod of his head, inviting, requesting that Sarah move toward the door and accompany him for lunch. With laughter, Sarah softened and walked toward Kolin. She crossed the threshold but immediately stopped as she stepped outside. Unknowingly Kolin was right on her hills so when she stopped just one step onto the sidewalk, after thinking about the fact that she still didn't know his name, she turned around nearly having her face buried in his chest because he was so close on her heels and not anticipating her stopping so abruptly.

"Just couldn't go another second, without being able to look at me huh?"

Kolin jokingly spoke with a chuckle. Um, that would be a negative! Sarah spoke firmly as she managed to pull back placing proper spacing between them.

Wait a minute, "I apologize," he spoke through a soft chuckle. It truly must be the fresh air because I promise you; this kind of behavior is not the norm for me. Please forgive me. I tell you what, let us just cross over to the other side of the street and start over. Are you open to that idea? For a few seconds Sarah gave it a thought, and though this time it wasn't heard, her stomach was still growling. She looked across the street being mindful of the, "food remedy" being at hand for her stomach and hunger then looked back at the stranger that she had now been entertaining in short playful conversation for nearly the last forty minutes. What do I do Lord, she silently thought as she looked back at him wanting to give the right reply. She softly sighed, and opened her mouth to speak when Kolin interrupt her thought speaking, "see look at that, here is our chance, traffic is at a complete standstill, in both directions. Come on, it is completely safe. He spoke as he gently shoved Sarah's shoulder with his forearm, encouraging her to walk with him. Sarah took a breath, and together they crossed the street.

Now safely on the other side of the street, Kolin took time to, formally introduce himself before entering the restaurant. "Okay, let's see if we can make this a comfortable lunch, with me being a stranger and all. So, "Mother Glenda's" assistant my name is Kolin Koole of K-3 Horizon, it is a pleasure meeting you. Excuse me. Forgive me, I was so focused on carrying out the instructions to come downstairs, I never asked your name, and Mother never gave it. Therefore, you are. "Ump," Sarah offered in response with both a "smirk and smile" mix of an expression. "Not enough hours in one day to answer that question she replied. Well okay then," Kolin chuckled, let us simply begin with your name then, how is that? He replied as he opened the door, waiting to enter after Sarah. Smart, Sarah Aakef she answered in laughter.

Hello Sarah Aakef, let this lunch meeting begin. Let us eat, a second longer and I am sure you would have passed out! I mean,

I would have passed out. Kolin laughed as he corrected his comment. "Are you joking me", Mr. Koole? Sarah asked with the shift of her eyes and a smile. Now Miss Aakef, we just met only seconds ago. I do not know you well enough to be, to use your words, "joking you". Especially since, that whole stomach growl thing happened many minutes ago over there on the other side of the street. Kolin spoke in laughter. Okay, so you really are, "joking me". Sarah replied. Okay, okay, okay I am Kolin confessed, but all in clean innocent fun. I promise you I mean no harm, so if it bothers you tell me and we will talk about the weather or something else dry and boring. You know what, I see right now that you are a character, if you are like this at work all day how does anyone around you get any work done.

Sarah's innocent comment reminded Kolin of his personal challenge and immediately erased the smile from his face. Okay, let us go ahead and put our order in. have you eaten here before Kolin politely asked. Wait a minute looks like it is now my turn to apologize to you. I am not sure what I said, but something is different in the atmosphere now and I apologize, for as you stated to me, I meant no harm, whatever it was.

Thank you Kolin spoke, but you said nothing wrong. On a personal note, I have had the opportunity to face, acknowledge, and address a few uneasy truths about myself, and for whatever reason, one of them just crossed my mind. However, you know what, I am gonna shelf that for now and we are going to place our focus on the matter at hand. "Is that so", Sarah asked, and what matter is that? This meeting and our growling stomachs, Kolin answered with a chuckle; and with that being said, mixed along with lots of great, give and take conversation, that is exactly what they did.

Towards the end of the meal, Sarah still was not sure why Mother Glenda had her to return. "Wait a minute Kolin; I am so playing right about now." Why do you say that, what are you talking about he asked. Kolin, when I leave her, I will either call Mother Glenda or drop by and see her personally. Now how can I when, I still have not confirmed the whereabouts of that envelope. Sarah answered. Um, good point how could you allow us to get so sidetracked like this. How dare you, lose your focus and selfishly feed your stomach on Mother Glenda's time like this? Kolin spoke with playful laughter as he continued to enjoy the remaining bites of his own meal.

Okay I see how it is going to go down Sarah replied as she used her cell phone to steal a shot of Kolin indulging on his meal. Thank you! She kindly yet firmly spoke, now I have proof if she has questions as to why it took us both so long to get back with her. "Are you kidding me", come on Sarah you would not really do that would you? Let me see you phone please. Kolin kindly asked. Okay sure, just a few seconds and I will let you see it. Sarah answered, just before emailing the photo of Kolin to her email address. Here, here you are Sarah offered. Wait, what did you just do Kolin inquired? Well for safekeeping, I emailed the picture to my email just in case it accidently erased. Here, here you go. Sarah spoke as she continued to offer her cell phone. Nah, I changed my mind. You keep it Kolin replied. Wow, you really gonna throw me under the bus like that.

Well, sounds like we might need separate checks. Kolin playfully spoke. "Nope, oh no we do not, this was your suggestion". You offered and promoted this luncheon so with that, automatically comes the bill. Sarah spoke assuredly with a sweet smile. Where did you get that one from Kolin asked. Oh, I did not have to go far at all for that one Sarah spoke. It came from me. You know as a child growing up my dad would sometimes say, "a closed mouth won't get fed," so to add to that I say, "a closed mouth won't get the bill," offer not and pay not Sarah spoke in laughter. So I see, so you are not an extender of an invitation if it means you are picking up the bill. No, I cannot say that's an "across the board" given. I am saying that this was your suggestion, invite and offer which equal out to be your bill. Sarah spoke with a soft smile. Okay Miss. Aakef, the next one is on you; there I am inviting me on a lunch with you sponsored by you the next time we meet. Whatever, you got jokes Kolin. Um, the next time, now that is funny. Go ahead, Kolin spoke. Go ahead and do what? Sarah asked. Go ahead and email that too, Kolin answered with a chuckle. You like that one, he asked. I do he continued reaching for his wallet to cover their bill. For a space of a few moments, the best that Sarah could do was smile, for right now, her normal wittiness seemed to escape her.

Okay Miss. Aakef, let us get back across the street locate this envelope and get Mother Glenda on the phone. Sounds like it might be a good idea for us to check in with her together. When the call attempt was unsuccessful, the two parted ways shortly after.

Whew, what an interesting day Sarah thought as she called checking in at the house to see if they needed anything that she could grab while she was out. After her wrapping up her call, her thoughts took her back to her day of errands and the chance to meet new people and share in conversation. The time she spent with the sweet little couple when delivering the lunch box was special she had to be honest with herself in recognizing that she truly enjoyed the awkward, yet playful and inviting lunch. She made a few short stops and was back on the road with home in view.

Let me try mother Glenda again, Sarah thought as she spoke the voice command into her cell phone. "Hello," mother Glenda answer, sounding, as she mostly sound when answering the telephone, as if she was in the middle of something. "Hello Mother Glenda, I just wanted to touch bases with you, this is

Sister Sarah." Oh, yes, yes dear, I have been expecting your call. Did you two locate the envelope? Wait a minute before you answer that let me ask, "Where are you right now my dear?" I am headed home. Why do you ask Sarah replied? I tell you what, Mother Glenda suggested lets hang up and you call me later on once you get home and have taken time to eat, get comfortable and unwind. I hope to have done the same by the time we speak again. Will you be able to do that? Sure, Sarah replied. Great, Mother Glenda spoke, Lord willing, we will catch up later on this evening. "Get home safely my dear", and with that being said there call ended.

Though challenged at times, and a few times side track by, wasteful fruitlessness. The "getting to know you," stage was finally at a point and place where Sarah was able to take her hands off, and release the reins to its rightful place. She knew that GOD's will and best always trumped anything she could humanly envision or conceive to be the best for her, but in times past she felt HE was too far away, too busy or a little tied up and wouldn't mind some of her assistance. Henceforth, resulting in, part of the last eight plus years of her, "life' investment". Which she would later find out, of her last "male distraction," was a one sided investment. Whew, but that was another thought, or rather "long story", for another day.

For Sarah knowing that it rained on the just and the unjust made it no easier to live out this particular life chapter. Why was it so hard for others to simply say what needed to be said when it needed to be said. Why were people so selfish careless and thoughtless when it came to matters of the heart and the feelings of others? Why couldn't she just meet someone with like convictions when it came to relationship, "why can't people honestly say, you are exactly what I want but I don't know if that's what I want right now?" she thought out loud.

Lord, please daily; help me to let go and let God, to completely forgive, and be moved not, to a place of bitterness or anger at the on site of any memory or thoughts of this, of him. Oh, not that I am looking, but for the man that you see fit to usher into my life, please God, help me receive him based upon "his" character, words and works, and not that of another from my disappointing past. Ump, Sarah sighed, surveying her past and present, "the work done, as well as that remaining to be done". She was open to change, but being single for some time now, she was sometimes, challenged, at trying not to control certain aspects of her life.

"Wow, God you know I can be a little opinionated and maybe somewhat stubborn, and possibly a little..., well never mind God, you already know this stuff, Sarah voiced with a smile. To make a long story short, just help me to be the "me" you created me to be in every way shape form and fashion, in every area and aspect of my life, being, and existence. Thank you for helping me to genuinely appreciate your great creation and look at others with eyes of compassion and the heart of You, I honestly pray; not my will Lord, but Your will be done in and with all things, Sarah Love Aakef."

Kolin Opens The Door

Unlike many times in the past, this time Kolin released himself to embrace, the uneasy and difficult task, of letting go, and "not" be in control. Finally, he was willing to face his raw thoughts and emotions. This meant having to address the knowns, as well as unknowns, along with past pain, hurt and fears. His wife had died an unexpected, untimely death, that alone was a hard truth to accept but Kolin knew before he could release past disappointments and hurts, he would have to deal with them.

Finally, he was willing to be open and honest with himself, and though it did not feel good being here in, and at this place, his anger had to be, dealt with. The more he gave room to his raw thoughts, emotions and feelings, the more he realized that it was not his wife or son that he was angry with, but God. Before totally releasing and addressing this harsh reality, Kolin pulled back.

"You know what, I don't have time for this," he spoke a loud as he grabbed his keys heading for the door realizing that he just needed to be somewhere else. For a short, Kolin drove with no particular destination in site. Every place he found himself seemed to be, "no place." He pulled off to the side of the road placing the gear in park as he rested his elbow against the door, using his left hand to prop his head on as he looked out over the steering wheel.

Who told him to cross this threshold, better yet, who told him to open this door? Before he knew it, he was holding his phone and making a call. It was a short conversation, almost ending before it truly began, and he was back on the road.

Now back on the road and rolling, Kolin had a particular place to be. Having arrived at his appointed place, he parked and went inside.

"There he is," a welcoming voice greeted as Kolin stepped inside. "Hey dad," Kolin replied with a chuckle as he embraced his father. "Come on in son, and let's see how well those protein shakes are working." His dad playfully spoke as they walked along. After changing, they spent the next 30 minutes or so working it out on an indoor tennis court. A game Kolin had grown to appreciate since the day his dad had placed a racquet in his hand. In a short time, he grew to become quite a talented player and like his dad, it afforded him the luxury of a full ride, all expense paid four-year college education. However, unlike his dad, Kolin declined the offer having no interest in the Tennis scholarship or furthering traditional schooling after high school. Instead, he continued to volunteer, take classes, trainings, gaining certifications when and where he could in the area of his passion, and for him it paid off. He found time to start and maintain a number of small businesses along the way.

Today's time with his dad was extremely therapeutic. He felt so honored and privileged to call this man dad. He talked, dad listened and shared, Kolin opened up, becoming transparent about the death of his wife, being a single dad, work, the life before, the life after, and the life now.

Kolin talked about the young lady who, had manage to catch his attention, and what it would take to start over, or if he even wanted to start over. After concluding there time with lunch Kolin, walked away with lots of great "food for thought." He now had more answers than questions, and though he still a little, in denial about becoming "stoic and somewhat cold," at least now he was awake. Now he was in tune enough to recognize, and know that he could not stay here in this drab mental, emotional and relationally closed place.

Kolin was open to being transparent, at the right time, and place, with the right people. He was going to intentionally, and actively work on recognizing and seizing, each moment, executing the necessary change, immediately and effectively. Starting today, he would be consistent at working on this transformation. "Boy, looks like I have my work cut out for me," he thought as he and his dad parted ways for the evening.

Is Kolin Ready To Live

Ready or not, Sarah Aakef had showed up. Like a streak of lightning, she had already penetrated the steel wall Kolin had placed around his heart. The more time they shared the warmer his heart had managed to become. The very thought of her gave him strength. "Wait a minute, what's up with this," he thought silently, what am I smiling about?" Before he could mask his inner thoughts, one of his contractors entered his office already in conversation mode about a current site. "Wait a minute, now that's a smile I haven't seen in a long, and I mean, a very long time," his contractor spoke. Care to share?" Being both surprised and a little embarrassed, all Kolin could manage was "yeah, I guess you caught me." Now, what were you saying Kolin asked as he cleared his throat? Following his lead, his contractor picked up right where he had dropped off in conversation when entering Kolin's office.

After many weeks of denial, refusal and avoidance, it was apparent and obvious, that he was undoubtedly hooked, being completely taken, and captivated by Sarah. As scared as he was of the thought of marriage and loving with all one has just to have it taken away, he really was willing, to be just that vulnerable again, and it was all because of Sarah. In addition, the fact that his little one was taken by her as well, was even more of a confirmation. "Ump," he thought, "what am I supposed to do with this? After holding back on so much for so long, how could someone love me, or trust their heart to me," he thought.

More Life More Sarah Unfolding

Spending time with Sarah, and taking in more family time had opened Kolin up to old memories and past friendships he had, unintentionally forgotten about. Growing up he would often hear his dad say, "one of the makings of a good person and businessman, is not in the "being able to be" part, but in the "actual being …" Depending on the conversational topic, the closing of this statement would, at times change. His father, not only told them to learn to possess a true appreciation for diverse people and cultures, but he lived it himself daily. This gave both Kevin and Kolin the seized opportunity to create and build friendships with young people of many diverse cultures, some of which they still kept in touch with to date.

At the time of his wife's death, and in his life after, a lot of Kolin's world became grey and cold but now he was looking out, over the canvas of life, deciding and choosing to have a better outlook, and life view.

Building and Creating - The Building

It still takes a village to raise a child, for some, sometimes family simply lives too far away. Nevertheless, Kolin had and utilized his family, especially his brother Kevin.

Kolin had learned to do some quick adjustments in some short amounts of time. It appeared that in years past all he'd received from his personal life were fast balls that leaves one no choice but to strike out. His favorite reply, "it's all good, I have it all under control", is what he'd become accustomed to offering whenever he was asked how he was doing. He seemed to be under the belief that he could go from, the busy, heavy, weighty, "devastation" of life while ending up right back at "hectic and weightiness," without a time of reflection, assessment, brokenness, release and or healing. Kolin believed that he could experience and endure all of this, and remain, reliable and effective, while enjoying a balanced, healthy quality of life. Well reality was on its way. Soon he would see and learn firsthand, just how possible this was; or rather, "was not".

Since abruptly, and bitterly becoming a single dad, Kolin expressed or had little interest in spending or sharing in family time. No one gets married, promising "I Do", already thinking about or looking at "Death Do Us Part". Why was he allowed to become so vulnerable with great dreams and hopes for the day and the future, to only wake up 36 short months later, forced to walk around with a huge hole in his chest while trying to parent a toddler. Un-resolves and bitterness filled most of his days as he went throughout the motion of work from day to day, almost daring someone to say something or question him.

All the men, and the three women, "who'd managed to make the cut", had taking note but was too intimidated to speak up about it. Kolin began his small contracting business in his senior year of high school. He had built a team of 20, well groomed and skillful, freshly, talented, wise, passionate, dedicated and resourceful people, who had never met a task or challenge they could not conquer, yet he was a different type of material when it came to his personal business and life. With his little one being so young, he leaned on family a lot. For the most part bedtime was really the bulk of his alone time with his little one. Those close to him knew that at some point, he would have to demolish the wall, find the balance, and show and share some soft, sweet, cuddly gentleness with his little one. However, right now, upon any opportunity that he could, he avoided it, daily he used all possible and available access and resources. Milking every possible angle until it was dry. Parenting was not a solo job and currently, he was dealing with lots of mixed emotions and feelings related to it.

Kolin Surveys Life

So many weekends Kolin spent filling his time with work, while having his little one spend time with his brother, Kevin or his parents. Though after his wife's death Kolin always managed to find a way out of family time at his parents' house, Kevin or Kathy were good about coming by to pick his little one up on their way to their parents. His toddler spent so much time with his brother family that he felt like a little brother to Kaye, and she looked forward to helping out with him whenever he was around. Just the thought of family time generated a smile, delivering it to his face, now that Kolin had been, released and awakened.

From the very beginning, it seemed that Mother Glenda had a way of helping Sarah, and Kolin as well, fill their spare time. Often, she had a volunteer opportunity or charity effort to fill or uphold. However, not every meeting or appointment required Mother Glenda's presence as much as it did Sarah's and Kolin's. With these two, a few minutes at a time easily rolled into hours. Days had rolled into weeks, and the weeks had unfolded into months.

Already, Sarah felt like home, and all those that mattered, not only could see it, but they felt the same way. She just fit. Kolin loved her, he loved her more than he thought possible, and his son simply melted like putty in her arms when the two met.

Now that he could see clearly, Kolin was ready to share the news. He had planned an evening at home with his family and to later be joined by a special guess. He had taken care of most of the preparations the prior evening having only a few things to finish up before the rest of his family arrived. Now that the whole gang had arrived, everyone were all seated after cleaned their hands, which gave Kolin the few minutes needed to apply his final touches to the meal. Of course, his mom unable to just have a seat and relax found her way to the kitchen to find something to do.

Kolin began by reminding his dad of the last meeting and long talk they had, explaining today's gathering had a lot to do with that meeting. He first shared with his family his love and appreciation for them and the way they had been there for him and his son and for both, allowing him to grieve in his own way, yet saying all the things they knew needed to be said, even the uneasy and not so welcomed stuff.

He shared how simply volunteering his knowledge and time to Mother Glenda over the last four months had ended up being a therapeutic blessing. Of course, by now the rest of the family was a captive audience because though his parents gave both he and Kevin JESUS growing up, thanks to work, Kolin's days and life had become too full and too busy for any, "GOD" thing. It had been that way since the death of his first wife.

Guys, there is so much that I could say right about now, but for the sake of time, let me just make this short, sweet and to the point. Working with mother Glenda on this non-profit project has been quite rewarding. Not only has it enriched my life, it has given me a reason to be in the presence of Mother Glenda and her husband the pastor, and to share in some passing conversations that, I later realized weren't just passing conversation. It was during this time that I was reminded of how my relationship or the lack thereof, with God is my responsibility. That if HE never does another, what I would label as, "a good thing," for me ever again in this life time that HE has already done more than enough, and way more than I could ever deserve. Nevertheless, even with the crazy busyness that I have made of my life, and turning my interest from God, HE still had my best interest at heart, HE still considered my need, and chose to bless me even still.

There is someone that I want you to meet, someone in which should be arriving shortly, someone that I hope you all will grow to adore and love as little man and I have, because I am planning to ask her to marry me. Eventually, we are going to need to sit down with you, Kolin spoke, as he pointed at Kathy. Sweetie, what did you just say? Kolin's mother asked." I said there is someone that I want you to meet that I plan…" Kolin's response was cut short by him excusing himself to respond to the doorbell but his instructions as he stepped away was for, "everyone to act natural," which was clearly heard by all.

Of course, sighs and grunts could be heard from the family, as Kolin headed for the door, leaving them behind in the kitchen. "Is he serious right now", his mom softly spoke. "Act normal, he said. Now upon the heels of such news, how are we supposed to do that with mounting unanswered questions, I mean does anyone know anything at all about this girl?" she continued. *Momma ~ K,* I just love you. You are soo genuine! Kathy spoke through an outburst of laughter, but for real though, what is normal, after an introduction like that, she continued jokingly.

It is simple, let us just look at this, as if we were being introduced to a new friend of Kolin's, Dad suggested. Good idea Kaye shared. Yeah, I guess we all are about to see how well that will go. Kevin softly spoke, before Kolin could return with his guest for the evening.

Having made it to the front door, Kolin was all smiles once he laid his eyes upon Sarah. Hey you, how was your ride over, Kolin asked. It was fine Sarah answered as she stepped inside, but I could have driven myself Kolin. I know you could have driven yourself, little miss independent, but then I would have missed out on the opportunity to drive you home, and wait a minute, didn't I just say hello to you, do we need to open the front door and start again, Kolin asked jokingly as he pointed to the front door.

Ump, okay you know what, I owe you an apology for that one, to answer your question, yes, you did say hello so let me take it back a little. "Well hello to you too sir, the ride over was just fine, but you know I could have driven myself right? Ha, ha ha, you just had to keep that part in there did not you. Kolin chuckled as he took Sarah by the hand escorting her to the kitchen with the rest of the family. Wait a minute, Sarah spoke as she stood still, pulling back on Kolin's hand. Sure, what is it Kolin asked as he looked back at Sarah a step behind. Just wait a minute; she spoke, then taking a pause withholding a soft worried look in her eyes.

Look it will be okay, he spoke before she could manage to speak any further. Listen, you are here in my home as my guest this is my home, and I invited you here because I want you here, so tonight we are in this together. Okay, so take a breath, relax and if you can't remember anything else throughout the course of this night, know that who and what you are, is more than good enough, so be comfortable in being, "simply you" because that is who I invited tonight. Now let us get in here and eat before we have another battle of the stomachs up in here! Kolin spoke with gentle laughter, while softly kissing her on her forehead yet firmly resting his hand around Sarah's shoulder to guide her, as they entered the kitchen together.

Kolin found her a comfortable seat in the middle of all of the family action, as he invited his mother over first. Mom, come on over here, mother I introduce to you Sarah Aakef. Sarah Aakef I introduce to you my lovely, thoughtful, sweet, beautiful, and wise beyond her years, mother. Full of warmth and all smiles Kolin's mother greeted Sarah. "Such a pleasure to meet you young lady, I look forward to getting to know you." Upon the ending of his mothers greeting, Kolin pulled his mother off, back over to the prep station in the kitchen, enlisting her help in getting the food to the table.

Okay, the rest of you guys introduce yourself, Sarah you've already met the little guy, so minus my brother-in law, this is everybody else, Kolin spoke as he did a sweeping motion with his arm to include all present in the room. His dad and Kaye jumped right in, followed by Kevin. When Kevin was done, Kolin's sister, pulled up a seat next to Sarah with Kathy, Kevin's wife leaning in against the countertop. The three girls chatted a few minutes while they waited to eat.

With everything in place and on the table, Kolin asked his dad to bless the food and soon after, dish by dish everyone enjoyed the prepared meal. It was a great evening. The family shared, "remember when" stories and played a few games generating lots of laughter the entire evening. Everyone, down to the little one donned a genuine smile.

Kolin was so, loving on his life and family right now, and though uneasy, and knowing he still had to deal with some unfinished feelings he felt grateful! "Thank you God, I so don't deserve to be in this space and place right now, but You ushered me here to this place anyway, even still, You gave me your best this is such a You thing, wow. Thanks God." Kolin silently thought, sharing a quick, personal moment with God.

Kolin's twin brother Kevin, along with his wife Kathy and daughter Kaye were the last ones to leave. His sister had left a little while prior to pick her husband up from the airport. With the food put away and the kitchen back in order, it was time to get Sarah home. Knowing that he would be Sarah's ride home later on that evening, Kolin had made prior arrangements for his parents to spend the night to give him the time he needed with Sarah.

Though it was late, Sarah's family just could not call it a night. They were still up and wide awake, almost watching the door, in anticipation of her return home. They were set, and ready to hear every detail of her evening with Kolin and his family.

When she finally arrived and stepped inside, almost in unison, her mom and sister T'wan asked, "how was it, how did everything go?" "Ha ha ha you guys got jokes, now go to bed." I will tell you all about it in the morning. Besides, with it being such a busy day, a sistah is tired! Sarah spoke as she continued on pass them and down the hall.

As quickly as Sarah had entered, she had disappeared down the hallway, and now totally out of sight, closing her bedroom door behind. T'wan and mom, looked at one another as T'wan expressed her disappointment of waiting up for Sarah to only be told to wait some more. Wow mom, guess we will have to get the "411" in the morning. I am mad at that thing! T'wan spoke with a chuckle. "Ump, yeeaaah!" Mom spoke, accompanied by lots of facial expression.

Just as they were allowing themselves to let go of the excitement of hearing about Sarah's evening, Sarah appeared shouting, "now y'all know I can't go to bed without telling y'all about tonight! Let me get the water going because this may take a while. "Coffee or Tea anyone, I am having Tea." T'wan and Mom put in their requests, and shortly after, they all sat around with their cups in hand, with all eyes and ears on the unfolding of Sarah's day.

Right now, if she believed in them, it would be easy for Sarah to believe that life was like a fairy tale. However, enough unfulfilled dreams and life expectations, had thrown and showed her the right amount of curve balls that most of the time, she possessed a somewhat, sour or bitter after taste behind, that was one fantasy that she was not gonna buy into. Though she wanted many more days and nights like this with Kolin and the rest of the Koole family, Sarah had not forgotten what betrayal, disappointment and hurt felt like. It takes a certain level of vulnerability and willingness to, "NOT" have, or be in control, to live out the type, and level of, "love relationship, and family lifestyle," that Sarah claimed to want. So now the question that she asked herself was, "am I willing to "risk" one more time, the possibility of investing the best of what is left of me, even at the chance of it later, proving to be a wasted investment?" Wow, how much do you want this Sarah, what risks are you open to and willing to take? She thought silently.

Why is Kolin here, God please help me, where is this going? The last thing I would want to happen is to meet and gain a great friendship to only later, lose it. Is this a seasonal, or lifetime, kind of thing? Well whatever and whomever, You have in store for Kolin's next life chapter bless them to possess a genuine care, compassion, concern and love for his son. Allow it to feel and be as if he was her very own, flesh and blood. He is too precious sweet and adorable to have anything less come into his life. Please place a special covering about him, shielding and protection him like only You can, in JESUS name I pray; Amen.

She's Such A Keeper

Heading in from an evening out, the "unsure" rain had made a decision. Consistent heavy rain now accented the sky. Whelp, so much for that wash you mentioned earlier, Sarah spoke. Wait a minute say that again, Kolin requested. The rain, surely you are not trying to wash your vehicle now, with all of this going on. Well actually, I think it is quite an opportune time if you ask me Kolin replied. Hump, whatever Kolin, whatever Sarah replied. No seriously, and it is no hit on the pockets, besides you cannot get any better than the source. Just think of it as God himself, hanging out with you helping you wash the car, Kolin teasingly spoke with a chuckle. Right Kolin, Sarah spoke with great doubt. So Sarah, are you in, or are you afraid of a little rain, Kolin challengingly asked. I hear you Sarah, somewhat cowardly replied. "Okay yes, you hear me but can I count you in, Miss.

Sarah", Kolin asked making direct eye contact. Silence was Sarah's immediate reply. Okay, you know what this task is not for the weak I tell you what when we get there I am going to pull into the garage to let you out, then get changed and take about 20 minutes to give the vehicle a quick wash off. Okay, Sarah replied.

Once they got to Kolin house he pulled into the garage, and unlike Sarah, she opted to exit the car before allowing him to get her door. She hurried inside, calling out for Kolin's dad. Kolin's parents were there at the house with his son while he and Sarah had been out. Mr. Koole, quick I need a full body rain suit or something water resistant to wear, she spoke as she worked on pulling her hair back out of the way. A water resistant suit, whatever for, Sr. Mr. Koole asked as he began his search to see what he could find. By now, Kolin was entering the house and calling out to his mom. "Shh", what is it sweetie she softly asked as she both answered and tried to get him to lower his voice. Oh, excuse me mom, is dad resting Kolin asked? No not dad dear, your son, and what are you two up to. First Sarah rushes into the house and now you. Yeah I know. Exactly where is Sarah?

Well before I shifted to park, Sarah was almost out of the vehicle. In addition, forget about getting her door. I didn't even have enough time to request to get her door. Like you, I would like to find out why she rushed into the house to. Oh, wow dear, did you say or do something? Before Kolin could give an answer, Sarah surfaced in a water resistant suit and ready for the rainy car wash.

Chop-chop cupcake, hurry up and go get changed, so we can knock this out! Quite surprised, Kolin was not sure if he should stop and ask questions or steal a moment to revel in the reality of Sarah's' spunkiness and willingness to such an odd task. You do realize that I am speaking, some time today right, Sarah asked as she softly brushed by Kolin asking if everything needed for the job would be located in the garage. Wait, he finally spoke, have a seat, allow me to change and catch up to you and we can then head out together. Okay, fair enough, Sarah spoke. I guess I can allow you a few minutes since I did, "sorta kinda" get the jump on you. Sarah spoke with a chuckle. Receiving her grace and allotted time, Kolin made haste. He managed to go change and resurface in what seemed like a flash. Well all right then, "let's do this," Kolin spoke allowing Sarah to lead the way to the garage. After mom, checked in on Kolin's son, she and dad found a window, which allowed them to take in the show. "Can you believe those two, Mrs. Koole spoke? To be honest, it looks like fun my dear, Sr.. Mr. Koole spoke. It looks like they are asking to be sick! She replied. Oh, so you do not remember, Mr. Koole asked his wife. Remember, remember what she asked. Mr. Koole whispered a short response in his wife's ear, but though brief he had obviously spoke a lot because she now wore a smile seeming to a span from one ear to ear. You are too much, she giggled, in response. You do not remember that day either, she replied. Oh, so I don't hum, Mr. Koole asked as he playfully bombarded his wife with smooches and tickles." There excitement and laughter could be heard from the window. Look at those two, Kolin spoke, I will have that again one day. As Sarah looked back to get a glimpse of her own, though with a genuine smile, she experienced both a refreshing and heart aching feeling all at the same time. A soft longing "wow" was the best that she could offer in response. Hey you two, come out and join the fun, Kolin offered as he called out to his parents waving and inviting them to join the rainy car wash. "No way," mom spoke with precise pronunciation, as she shook her head from left to right to confirm her no. "Why not", Mr. Koole asked. So sweetie, are you telling me, you are for that craziness outside, his wife asked? "Sure, why not" he replied. Well what about the baby, she asked? I think he will be fine Sr. Mr. Koole answered. How about we just, look, he offered kindly pulling his wife along.

Look at him, he spoke as they stood in the doorway of the bedroom where there young grandson rested. We have at least ten to fifteen minutes, and if it makes you more comfortable, we can set an alarm on my watch or cell, what do you say, are we going outside to join the kids, he asked? "What am I going to wear", his wife asked. Well let us find something Mr. Koole encouraged. Okay, but set the alarm first his wife requested. Which one the watch or cell he asked. Both, I rather be safe than sorry she answered. Sr. Mr. Koole, set a ten minute alarm on both his watch and cell and after a short search both momma and poppa Koole had located something fitting for the occasion and where outside alongside Sarah and Kolin in the rain.

Kolin was open to, and getting excited about the idea of marriage. When he married his first wife, "As long as we both shall live" carried a decade upon decade, upon decade of weight with him. During that time, Kolin gave all that he had to the "We, Us, and Our," life Chapter. His wife had pledge the very same. Therefore, there was no question, about a family and planned future. Now fast forwarding to his current day, and once again, he was ready to pledge all that he had and more. Quite some time had passed, since he had talked to Him, but in the last year or so, Kolin had taken a lot more time out for talks with God. He intentionally sought Him on, "all things Kolin." Though hard for him to do, Kolin was open, as well as willing to trust God again, to grant Him an invitation with all access to his life and it was a great feeling. He had long forgotten how much his relationship, "the one he used to openly share with his wife" meant to him. It was a saddening thought to think how he had refused to think about it. However, he now had a seized second chance at having a "help meet," and he was truly grateful. Where there was once anger, bitterness, resentment, and guilt, he now embraced and possessed forgiveness, compassion, love and peace. He was grateful for the time spent with his first wife and now found that, once again, he was considering speaking those seven words, "As long as we both shall live," I guess love and life is for the living he softly spoke. "Love and life is for the living." I totally release myself to extend and receive love the way you intend Lord, the way YOU intend. Thank you for bringing Sarah Aakef into my life and the life of our son, for just as, "I Did" years ago, once again I have an "I do" opportunity and with your blessing I am going to embrace it, seize it, extend it, share it and live it out. May our son and Sarah ever and always feel love in our home, and wherever our son's travels may take him, please God, ever go and stand with him, leading and directing him in and with all things. My parents did it with me now I do it with my son. I give KJ back to You. I trust that You can, and will protect him God, so please do it like only You can.

Thanks to Mother Glenda, Kolin met Sarah, and from that day forth his attitude and life was ever changed. Though they enjoyed lending a hand to a few great causes along the way, it also afforded them the seized opportunity to grow a great friendship and get to know each other a lot better. He was big on balancing out being both a contributor as well as a consumer to the world around him, that which he was able to reach, touch and change for the better. These efforts were exactly what Kolin needed, and the best way to get to know Sarah, and see her enter act in some of the areas that meant a lot to he and his family. Kolin was serious, something in him opened up that day in that playful conversation with Sarah upon their initial meeting and now, any time spent around and with her, was a matter of gathering, processing and finalizing. If it continued to go along as it had thus far, Sarah too, would soon Kolin's intentions for her, was marriage. Whatever was left of the rest of his life, he wanted to live it out with Sarah and he was already arranging some of the behind the scene aspects to make that a reality and with Gods kiss of approval it would be so. Either way, time was soon to reveal it all.

Kolin was totally trusting God with this one, and though some of the chatter around him wondered if it was too soon to propose such a commitment, his family was supportive, and in and with that he had peace.

Ump, he softly snickered within, "now what?" With this fresh on his mind, he immediately gave his sister-in-law Kathy a call, and within a short, he was ending the call.

Kathy had been present that evening, some time ago, when Kolin had invited Sarah over for a meal with the family, and though he had made his intentions clear to the family then, she still was not quite expecting the short, yet very informative conversation she'd only seconds ago shared with her brother-in-law. She was all smiles as she thought of her brother-in-law being open to dating, believing in, finding and receiving love all over again. He had grown so much over the course of the passing months. This truly was an awakening for him. Better yet, it was a seized awakening, and she along with the rest of the Koole family was happy and excited about where it was taking him.

Wow, Sarah truly taught him. He is actually ready to, "all the way," do this. "Ump, such a blessing, she thought a loud! Man I tell ya, "They That Wait", she softly spoke. Ump, "They That Wait."

About the Author

Delanda McNair is a North Carolina native born 4th of 5 children. Her father, though a man of many paid hobbies, was a part-time county sheriff and a full-time electrician for one of the main employers in their hometown. Her talented and gifted mother was a seamstress. Though a small town raising, both intentionally and quite uniquely, her parents humbly gave them **big time** life and lots of love.

A Note To My Reader

I seize this opportunity to personally thank you for reading

YOU Taught Me, please be sure to post your review on Amazon.

And share the book and or title with your friends or favorite book club!

www.ingramcontent.com/pod-product-compliance
Lightning Source LLC
Chambersburg PA
CBHW031310280626
47169CB00017B/1179